Minky Robinson

CHAIR

TRAVELLER

ISBN: 9780648187714 - paperback

A catalogue record for this
book is available from the
National Library of Australia

Minky Robinson

CHAIR

TRAVELLER

BY

ANGELA MOYLE

Other works by Angela Moyle

Capital Adventures children's picture book series
- Phoebe Digs Politics
- Clyde's Prickly Ride
- Hope's Dawn Service

Minky Robinson young adult series
- Minky Robinson: Chair Traveller
- Minky Robinson: Secrets Unlocked
- Minky Robinson: No Love Lost

For my ancestors - without whom this story would never have been dreamed up!

ONE

I've always known my life was strange. I know that's an odd thing to say, but you couldn't exactly say my life was all that normal. To start with, I was given one of the weirdest names on the planet. If I had a dollar for every time someone told me they'd never known anyone with my name, I would have enough money by now for a decent holiday to Disneyland.

My surname is Robinson. I will freely admit that part of my name is not so bad. I guess you could say it's the part my dad gave me. My dad is Matthew Robinson and he is a pretty awesome guy. He is the polar opposite of my mother, Jennifer Robinson nee Taylor who is the evil creature who gave me my first name... Minky.

What's wrong with Minky you ask? Ok, I'll play along and pretend you didn't cringe when you first heard it. If you've given it more than two seconds thought though you would have already come up with at least one or two of the nicknames I have tirelessly suffered through my whole school life to date. 'Stinky Minky' would be up there as both the most common and definitely the less imaginative on the list.

Not only does Minky sound like it is a kind of whale or the fabric you would make a baby quilt out of, it also sounds more like some kind of nickname (a nickname for what I don't know), but to me it sounds so unsophisticated and it's always felt like my silly name has never done anything to help me out in life, it's only ever held me back.

It doesn't help that it is not a very common name. I don't know anyone with the name and I've never ever seen it on something like a mug, keychain or trinket at a gift shop, unlike all the nice normal names like Mia, Elizabeth, and Amy.

It makes me cross that my mother decided to give me such a hideous name. I guess because she never had to deal with a problem name, she doesn't fully comprehend the suffering she's put me through every day of my thirteen years of life. My mother was christened Jennifer Taylor. The only complaint she ever had with her name was that she often had to contend with at least one, but sometimes several other 'Jennifers' in her class at school and now as an adult she still has the same problem at work, which is usually solved by one of them using different variations, for example, Jen, Jenny or Jennifer.

I tend to avoid having frivolous or unnecessary conversations with my mother, but over the years when other people have asked her where she came up with the name Minky, I have to admit, I have listened in to try and understand why.

Her story goes that Minky was a name she thought of while she was at university and she knew if she ever had a daughter, she would give her that name. I've always wanted to ask her what drugs she was taking while she was at uni, but I don't think that question would go down too well with her.

Lets put the name thing aside for a bit and say that even if she hadn't given me the worst name on the planet, my mother and I would still not be friends.

Five words I'd use to describe Jennifer Robinson:

Supercilious

Opinionated

Infallible

Uppity

Workaholic

You might think I am being a bit harsh saying such things about my mother, but that is another word I could use to describe her. 'Harsh'. In my mind, she and I are like chalk and cheese.

The only time I really get mad at my dad is when he says Jennifer and I are so similar and that's why we clash.

If there were five words to best describe me, I think they would be:

Awkward

Invisible

Self-conscious

Under-average and thanks to my name…

Unsophisticated.

To add insult to injury, I'm not the only child in this family scenario. When I was ten and had finally accepted I was going to be an only child for the rest of my life, to my utter embarrassment, my parents decided to go and bring another baby into this world. When all my friends' mothers were well and truly done with having babies, my mother was swanning around looking like she'd eaten a basketball for lunch.

As much as I hate to admit it though, it took less than two minutes after meeting my little baby brother Zachary, for me to fall hopelessly in love for the first time. He really was, and indeed still is the cutest child I've ever met, with a generous mop of dark hair, and dimples visible from birth. I think for the rest of his life, he will have everyone he meets smitten with him from the get-go.

Zac's five-word description would be:

Angelic

Memorable

Handsome

Charming

Popular

What? You want to know how a three and a half-year-old can be popular? Well, based on the number of play dates he regularly has, I worked out once Zac literally has more friends than me, so from my perspective, he gets to own the popular label out of the two of us.

My dad is the older version of Zac. He's charming, affable and the sweetest man I know. As mentioned previously, his name is Matthew Robinson. Most people call him Matt, some call him Matthew but I always call him Dad.

My mother is a career driven solicitor and a no-nonsense one at that. If she wasn't so intent on furthering her law career, the big family move never would have happened.

You see, when Jennifer was offered this great job overseas in Dubai, she couldn't pass it up and when she has her mind set on something, nothing will get in her way from success.

I tried. I really tried to stop her from plucking her children from the only home they'd ever known in Canberra and dumping them in some foreign city literally on the other side of the earth and in the middle of a desert.

You could say it was a battle of the stubborn Robinson women and as far as battles go, I wasn't completely defeated. I am claiming a half win. It's only a half win because we all did end up moving from our home in Canberra. Jennifer, Dad, and Zac moved to Dubai and her solution for me was to send me to Sydney to live with her parents.

Somehow, Jennifer managed to get me into the same school she attended when she was a girl. The school is called Stone Park and it's a very old and elite co-ed private school in inner Sydney. It has a waiting list a mile long to get into it, so it surprised everyone when they found a spot partway through the school year for little ol' insignificant me.

It could have been because Jennifer is an alumna. It might have a little to do with her very discretely helping them out of a legal problem here and there over the last few years, but I think it's mainly because she has contributed lots of money to their many fundraising events.

My new roommates (my mother's parents) are two local legends in their little corner of Sydney. They go by the names Leanne and Robert Taylor, they are also known as Lea and Bob, but when dealing with me they answer to Nan and Pop. They're both in their mid-sixties now but are very much tied to their job so I don't see them slowing down and retiring anytime soon.

They live and work in an old antique and collectables shop in Newtown. It is the home my mother and her sister Cass grew up in which is kind of odd for me to think about. What's even stranger is Pop grew up there too so I guess it's got a lot of my family history wrapped up in that unique home.

My mother rarely ever told me stories about growing up on the busiest street in Newtown in a pokey two bedroom apartment above an antique shop, but I guess it's fair to say I probably wouldn't have shown any interest in hearing about it if she had.

My pop loves to tell a yarn, driving around in his '55 Chevy convertible and pretty much all the old things in his shop. If you get him talking about his antiques or old cars then good luck getting away. He's quite old fashioned and isn't one to embrace change. I think the only change that has occurred in his life that he admits was for good was when they installed a flushing toilet inside the shophouse and stopped having to use the old outhouse in the backyard. I've always agreed, that change seemed like a win for everyone.

Nan is a real sweetheart. She works very hard at keeping Pop happy and well fed, and you couldn't fault her on either account. Nan constantly potters around the house, keeping it as neat as you can keep an overfilled tiny little home, and she also spends a lot of time working in the shop helping Pop out. She does all the bookwork and she also tends to customers.

When I was little I loved visiting my grandparents. You would have to admit, having an interesting place like an antique shop to spend hours getting lost in among the old treasures and poking around finding random and unusual things sounds pretty cool. The last few years, however we really hadn't visited them much, and once Zac was born, because of the dire lack of space in the apartment, when we had visited Sydney, we normally stayed at a motel a couple of blocks away and didn't tend to spend that much time in the shop.

The shop has the very original name of 'King Street Antiques and Collectables'. Being an antique and collectables shop on King Street in Newtown I'd say they definitely didn't leave any room for ambiguity with that name. At least the name isn't offensive or unsophisticated like someone else's I know (just saying).

It was actually Pop's parents who originally bought the building and set it up with the antique shop downstairs and residence upstairs. Pop always said it would be unlucky to rename it although my personal opinion on the matter is he just isn't one for change.

Probably the thing I love most about the shop is that it connects to the family home and if it hadn't been for the staircase at the back that led to the small upstairs apartment, you wouldn't know where the shop ended and where the house began. Both the shop and the house are filled to overflowing with so many old and delectable goodies. It wouldn't be an exaggeration to say everything in Nan and Pop's house is just as eclectic and interesting as the items they have for sale in the shop.

If truth be told, it amazed me to think my mother had ever lived in a place with so much character and soul. Our house in Canberra had crisp white walls throughout and although it was generous in size, it was very plain and quite sparsely decorated. The complete opposite of the shophouse, which was small, and over decorated. I guess perhaps the Canberra house reflected the way Jennifer likes to keep her life, highly organised, predictable and boring. Leave anything out of its proper place, and she'd hit the roof. Even poor little Zac learnt at a ridiculously young age he couldn't leave his toys strewn around the house and messy eating was unacceptable.

Initially, I admit, I didn't like the idea of moving to Sydney and the thought of starting over in a new school, particularly a school with a reputation like Stone Park, absolutely terrified me.

I had to start from scratch again in the friend making area (which as discussed previously has never really been my strongest ability).

There were a few things that surprised me about my big move though. First of all, I had to admit, the initial few days of my new private school were not as bad as I imagined they would be. Unlike how it was when my mother and Aunty Cass attended Stone Park. The school now has a very large multicultural population, which definitely helped me out with my unusual name problem. Along with all the kids at Stone Park with trendy names such as Flame, Mercedes, Spirit, and Dido, I don't think I saw one person even blink an eye when Minky Robinson was introduced. Name dilemma seemingly diverted.

The second surprise was how easy it was to make several nice friends. I guess because my school in Canberra was so small, everyone knew everyone, and we didn't get a lot of new people. I'd been there so long, and knew everyone so well, I didn't think I would know how to make a new friend.

Although Stone Park is known for its academic achievements (again, this has never been a strong point for me), they also encourage students to join one or more sports programs. This was actually really exciting for me because we didn't have many sports teams at my old school and the ones we had were mixed so I was often the only girl on the team and not given much of a go. With enthusiasm, I joined the girl's netball, softball and hockey teams and after proving I had above average skills in each of those sports, I was quite quickly accepted and even made a few friends in each.

Don't get me wrong, there were still stuck up and snobby, cliquey kids at the school, but maybe because it was so much bigger than the one I'd grown up with in Canberra, I was able to blend in a bit better and not stick out so much which honestly was a-okay with me.

So this is how I came to live in my mother's old bedroom, the one she shared with her sister when she was a kid, in a small two bedroom apartment above an antique shop on a busy, bustling Sydney street.

Even though I'd left the only home, school and city I had ever lived in, was no longer living with my parents and it had all happened in a matter of weeks, things were not as bad as they could have been. Anyway, I'm not going to complain, if all these things hadn't happened, I would never have found 'the chair'.

Two

"Reg said you can find the shop on *The Google* now." Pop said eating his breakfast with his eyes glued to the morning newspaper.

"That Google machine is a marvel Darl. How does it know?" Nan said as more of a statement than a question.

I'd been living with Nan and Pop for only two weeks but we'd all settled into a good routine. I figured out pretty quickly they were creatures of habit, but I had to admit, I was really enjoying most of their habits so I couldn't complain.

I loved eating meals together at the small round table just off the kitchen. It was never done when I lived with my parents. Zac had his own meal times, I ate when I could between different sports, Dad would eat with either Zac or I but no matter when we ate it was always right in front of the TV with it turned on.

I couldn't remember the last time Jennifer ate with us at home. Her work hours usually meant she had left before I was up and didn't get home until dinner was safely consumed.

My grandparent's cute Google conversation made me smile. I knew they didn't like me using electrical devices at the table, but it was Saturday morning so they were a bit more relaxed. I had my iPad mini next to my cereal bowl while I ate, kind of like the modern-day version of Pop scouring over his newspaper. We were both engrossed in what we were reading, except I was checking Facebook not reading the news.

I closed the Facebook app and did a quick Google search for 'King Street Antiques and Collectables', and wasn't surprised when all that came up was the location on King Street in Google Maps, a picture of the front of the shop with the sign all blurred out on Street View and their phone number and opening hours presumably from the Yellow or Whitepages listing.

"You know, if you guys ever want to get a real online presence, say a website, Facebook page or Instagram, I'd be happy to be your social media manager," I offered.

"Mgh! We don't need any of that, I just said we're already on *The Google* now. Besides, people who love collecting and antiquing are hunters and detectives. It's about the thrill of the find… we wouldn't want to make it too easy for them." Pop said with a wink.

I thought about the shop downstairs overflowing with things. There was so much stuff it was almost like an episode of *Hoarders*, except Pop knew exactly what he had and he would only keep things he could get good money for, not just any old junk. When I was younger I used to ask him about certain objects down there. I'd laugh when Pop got all serious and turned into one of the expert appraisers from *Antique Roadshow*. Not only did he usually know about the item, he also had a knack for knowing where it had come from and sometimes even knew a fun fact or story about it.

"Do you have plans today Minky?" Nan asked as she cleared my empty cereal bowl from the table.

"Not anymore. I was meant to be playing netball today, but I just got a text to say it's been cancelled due to the weather." All three of us looked out the nearby window at the dark and menacing clouds, generously drenching the city.

"Well, looks to me like good weather to stay inside." Pop said, "Saturdays are busy in the shop though, so if you're going to be down there, try not to get in the way."

"Yes'r!" I said saluting him playfully.

About an hour later I was showered and changed into my favourite jeans and a comfortable t-shirt, and made a half hearted effort to run the brush through my unruly hair. I didn't go to too much effort because I wasn't expecting visitors or planning to even leave the shop.

I updated my Facebook, just in case anyone was interested in hearing me moan about my netball game being foiled by the weather and I followed through on my plan to head downstairs and browse the shop for treasures.

Saturday may have been their busy shop day, but to me, it looked pretty dead. It could have been the storm keeping people at home I guess but aside from me and Pop, there was no one else in the shop at all.

The bell above the front door chimed as someone walked through. I couldn't see the door from where I was, but I could faintly hear the voices and from what I could make out, it wasn't a customer it was one of Pop's closest and oldest friends, Colin Murphy. Col, like Pop still lives in the house he grew up in, which is only a hop, skip and jump away from King Street. He is now retired and is always hanging around. He most likely just popped in for a chat with Pop.

"G'day Minky," Col said with a cheeky twinkle in his eye when he spotted me. Col and Pop grew up together and in our family, he was always thought of as a bit of a scallywag. It was said in a nice way, but it was easy to see he enjoyed teasing and ruffling feathers with some of his comments.

"Hello, Mr Murphy."

"Please, Darl, it's Col. No need for formalities with me." He winked. "What kind of mischief are you up to today?"

"Netball was cancelled because of the storm. So I thought I'd just poke around the shop. I haven't really had a proper look around here since I moved in."

"Sounds like a brilliant idea. Have you found anything special yet?"

"Just make sure you don't mess things up Minky," Pop said. "And for heaven's sake, don't break anything."

"Ah, kids'll be kids Bob, let her cut loose a bit and have some fun."

"Well you'd be an expert on that Col, you're the biggest kid I've ever met." The two old men continued to give each other a bit of a jab, so I used that cue to leave them be.

I focused back on scourging and snooping around, there was seriously so much stuff in the place. I knew if I rummaged the whole day it wouldn't even be the tip of the iceberg.

Even though I loved the idea of the shop when I was younger, I'm sure the stories and the actual items had been lost on me. Now I was older and more mature, it was very cool, and everything seemed a lot more meaningful like they all had an actual purpose.

The deeper I got into the back corner of the shop, the muskier it smelt. Everything was arranged all higglty-pigglty, and as I got further back it was even more like an unsorted dumping ground.

I'd never been brave enough I guess, to venture this far into the back. Aside from the smell back there, it was also quite dark and the thought did occur to me if there was a haunted area of the old shophouse at all, it would be in that gloomy corner.

I could hear a full on storm now raging outside and thunder was cracking loudly, but it was such a hidden back corner, the lightning didn't seem to reach that area to help light it up. I couldn't help but think an electrical storm seemed like the perfect time to investigate such a spooky space. Better to scare myself in the daytime while the shop was open and people were around than late at night.

Now, I know this is going to sound completely cliché… but it was right at this moment when I first laid eyes on the chair.

THREE

There was an unassuming charm about the old armchair I found in that musty back corner. On any other day, I may not have even given it a second glance, but today seemed like the perfect time and place to find such a treasure and I was unexplainably drawn to it. I would say it was almost like the Red Sea of antiquey things parted, trumpets sounded and there at the end in the dark corner of the shop with a spotlight bearing down on it was an old mystical chair full of intrigue and drama. Ok, I might be exaggerating a little, but it really did pull me in.

This is where you catch me out about the parting of the antiquey Red Sea, because the actual truth is, it wasn't easy to get to. I had to really squeeze my way through all the stuff. I shimmied past an old Singer sewing machine with a beautiful iron treadle peddle, a set of almost pristine Encyclopaedia Britannica's from 1968 stacked in a precarious pile, lots of boxes and some other bits and pieces that all seemed to have an impressive layer of dust on them. The chair wasn't in the best state of its life. It certainly looked like at some stage it had been greatly loved, but the leather attempting to cover it was now dry and cracked and was so worn in places you could see the wire springs and horse hair padding wanting to peep out.

I grabbed a crocheted napkin I found on a cedar buffet nearby and used it to give the chair a bit of a dust down. It was only after some inspection and testing to make sure it wasn't going to collapse that I lowered myself down on it like I was a queen sitting on her royal throne.

Even though it wasn't in perfect condition, as I wiggled around in it, I noticed it was actually quite comfortable. It seemed like the perfect chair to settle down with a good book. I decided I'd had enough of the antique hunting. I knew I had a very long day ahead of me so this chair was going to help me survive a dreary stuck inside kind of day.

I remembered earlier in the week I had found a box of interesting looking books in one of Nan and Pop's storage cupboards upstairs. I wangled myself out of the back corner and sped upstairs to grab a book or two to read in my new discovery.

I quickly and easily found the box of books in the exact spot I'd seen them. They were all pretty old, and when I'd first come across them, I didn't have the time or inclination to check them out properly. Now I had hours to kill, they were going to help me slaughter those hours. I sifted through them feeling a little like I was going through a treasure chest searching for gold. *Beasts of Bakersfield, Magnificent Seven,* as I dug deeper the books seemed more worn, bigger and definitely for younger kids, babies even. Rather than spend another second rummaging through them, I decided to grab a generous pile and headed back down to my comfy chair. Nan was vacuuming the lounge room, just part of her normal Saturday morning routine. She stopped me on my way back down to the shop.

"You've found your pop's old books Minky?" she asked although it was less of a question, more of a statement. I nodded and gave her a grimace that silently said please don't say I shouldn't be reading them.

Now I'd decided on my activity for the day, I didn't want my book reading plans to be foiled. Nan seemed to realise this without me saying anything. She softened and said. "I'm sure Bob won't mind you reading them, just so long as you're careful, and remember to put them back where you found them when you've finished. Just keep in mind, when you take things into the shop they run the risk of being sold."

"I will!" I called excitedly as I raced back down the stairs and did my shimmy dance back into the corner to the waiting chair.

My first problem then presented itself. Although the chair was comfy and the worn out arms were perfect for resting a book and curling into, there really wasn't enough light to read in that dank corner. I thought about whether I could move the chair, but it seemed pretty heavy and there was absolutely no way in the world that could happen with the all junk, I mean stuff, that was all piled around it.

I knew there was a table lamp right near the front counter I thought would be good for reading under. It was an ugly old brown thing with tassels that hung around the edge of the shade.

Thankfully though, before I had a chance to go find and bring the lamp over to the chair corner, I realised it was a plugin lamp, and it would be easier to find a needle in the shop than to find a power socket to plug the old lamp into.

I thought about looking for a torch, but in the end I decided even if there wasn't enough light to read the fine print of a novel, there was probably just enough light in the area to see the pictures of a picture book, so I grabbed what looked like the oldest book from the bottom of the book pile and settled back into the comfy old chair.

The book was very worn and the spine was tattered, it was old after all, but it wasn't just that it had survived a lot of years, it looked as though it had been a very well read and well-loved book. I studied the aged cover. It was very retro and adorably old-fashioned, obviously a book for little kids. I loved the gorgeous, colourful illustrations on the cover, it had a sweet playful puppy, a kitten with a big blue bow around its neck and a fluffy yellow duckling. Printed in big black bold capital letters was possibly the longest book title I had ever seen on a children's book. THE LITTLE DOG WHO FORGOT HOW TO BARK AND THE LITTLE BOY WHO FOUND HIS FORTUNE.

I opened it to the first page and noticed there was something written on the inside of the cover. Finding a snippet of light I managed to read the inscription made out in lovely neat handwritten cursive *For our first grandson Robert. Love Grandpa and Grandma. 1948'*. I now understood why these books might be special to my Pop. They were his very own books from his childhood. This one was probably given to him around the time he was born.

I'd never even really thought much about Pop having parents let alone grandparents. I'm sure they probably died many years before I was born, but it did make me wonder what they'd been like, and of course what Pop would have been like as a small child reading his picture book and being nursed by grandparents that no doubt doted over him, as grandparents tend to do.

It was a bit of a mind bend for me, but none of that had ever occurred to me until I saw the inscription in the book.

My fingers traced over the carefully printed inscription that had been penned more than half a century ago and as I did, I continued to imagine my pop as a toddler, enjoying the book and the bright coloured pictures most likely even before he could read.

Now, this is the part of my story you might have some trouble swallowing. Well, don't worry, I'm not sure I was ready to eat any of it myself.

With absolutely no warning, the heavy darkness that was surrounding me was overwhelmed by a brilliant flash of light.

I'd never encountered anything like it. A million thoughts came to my mind at that split second moment and to say I was scared was an understatement. There wasn't really any time to react though, it all happened so fast. The only explanation I could think of for what had happened to me was… I'd somehow been struck by lightning.

Four

Even though the chair didn't seem to be moving, it felt like everything around me was. It was like I was attached to an agitator in a very big, bright and high-speed washing machine. I tried to let out a scream, but either nothing came out, or the sound was instantly swallowed up by the light.

Then as quickly as the flash commenced, it ceased and all the rush and movement stopped and it felt like I'd landed with a heavy thud.

While the movement feeling happened, I had curled myself up in a foetal position on the chair and was now clutching the baby book as though it was able to somehow protect me.

Slowly lifting my head up and looking around me it was like a completely different day. The sun was streaming through the window and there was not a cloud in the sky.

Part of my fear ebbed away as I was comforted by the cheeriness of the beautiful day and the familiar space. It didn't ease my heart-rate at all. I could feel it thumping at a double rate through my chest.

For a few seconds, in my stunned fear, I didn't question my surroundings and then as quickly as I had started to relax, I remembered I had just been in the gloomy, cluttered, dust filled shop and even though I knew I was still at 'King Street Antiques and Collectables', I wasn't in the shop anymore. I had somehow been transported upstairs to my bedroom.

Even though everything happened so quickly, in many ways it felt a bit like things were moving in slow motion as my mind kept flipping from sheer terror to a strange sense of comfort.

I was definitely in my upstairs bedroom at Nan and Pop's place, but it looked so different. The wallpaper was the same, but instead of being very pale, worn out yellow, it was actually a lovely vibrant lemon colour and the wallpaper was fresh and new, none of the edges had curled like they had in my current room.

In the place where my bed was supposed to be, was a lovely crisp white chest of drawers and in the position my desk usually held just under the window, was a white babies cot.

My legs felt like jelly as I very shakily and slowly stood up. I looked down and marvelled at the old style but fresh looking carpet under my feet, very different to the carpet in my bedroom now.

I was still clutching the book when I bravely peeped over the top of the cot and looked down at the sleeping chubby faced baby boy who was asleep in the bed. His delightfully tiny but pudgy right hand was protectively resting on a book. A book that looked very much like the book I had in my hands, only this one looked almost brand new.

You are going to think I am crazy and remember, I have a baby brother, so I know better than most kids my age, the last thing you ever want to do is disturb a sleeping baby. It's like the equivalent of waking a hungry dragon from a hundred year sleep, no one except the bravest (or indeed the silliest) souls would dare do it.

I don't know why I did it. I already knew in my gut the book under the sleeping baby's hand was going to have the same inscription in the cover as the one I was holding, but it was as if I just had to see it with my own eyes to make sure.

I slowly tried pulling the book away from his grasp but wasn't counting on his chubby, sticky hands catching on it from his sleepy sweat. As I inched it away he gave a little start and when his hand flew up, I bravely snatched the book up. Before I could check the inside cover though, I watched in horror as his little fists went up to his eyes and I froze like a deer in the headlights, desperately wishing for a place to hide as he rubbed his eyes sleepily. When his eyes popped open he wore a dreamy smile as he gave a stretch as though he had woken from a very satisfying nap.

Without a doubt, he would have been expecting the big person standing over his cot to be his mum or at least someone he knew. The last thing he would have been expecting would have been the strange girl he had stealing his precious book away from him.

I would have guessed him to be anywhere between the age of 12 to 18 months old and in a lot of ways, he reminded me of my little brother Zac. The resemblance was actually quite amazing. It could be because all babies look the same though with their chubby cheeks, big wide set eyes and gummy mouths.

It felt like longer, but it was probably less than ten seconds we both stared at each other with big eyes and a dumbfounded look. I gave him an awkward smile and little wave but quickly realised his countenance was one that was all too familiar to me. It was the face a baby makes when they are about to scream their neighbourhood down.

"Shh, bubba." I tried to hush him with a whispery cheerful voice, knowing in my gut I was way too late to stop the onslaught. I put my hand out towards him to give him a friendly reassuring pat, but unfortunately, it only made things worse. He wasn't impressed with me touching him and his loud howl very quickly turned into a blood-curdling scream.

To my horror, underneath his screams, I heard the familiar sound of footsteps on the creaking floorboards heading towards the room. I frantically looked around for a place to hide, but aside from the chair, that didn't actually belong in the room, there really wasn't anywhere I could go.

It was too late anyway, there was a cheery voice approaching the door that was already shushing to settle the baby and a second later the door flew open.

I threw my hands up in surrender as if I was caught doing something very wrong and was about to be taken down.

I'm sure I have never worn a more terrified facial expression in my life as I was confronted with the woman.

We both stood there frozen, staring at each other.

FIVE

There was nothing normal about what was happening, but until I saw the woman, it didn't properly click with me that I could be in a completely different time zone or dimension. In fact, putting some of the puzzle pieces together, it made me think I had somehow ventured back to about the time the inscription in the book had been written, around the late 1940s.

The woman looked like a character out of an old movie or one of those old shows my Nan watches on the ABC. She wore a calf-length blue pencil skirt, crisp white shirt neatly tucked into her skirt and a pretty red cardigan.

Her hair was wavy and quite stylish but nothing like what you would see these days. I remembered Nan once talking about 'setting' her hair when she was a kid and I figured this kind of style might have been what she was talking about.

I've never been very good at working out someone's age once they were older than a teenager, an adult is an adult to me really, they're all old. It might have been because I'd been living with an older generation, but this adult seemed pretty young. Younger than I can ever remember my mother being.

If I put myself in the place of the beautiful young lady, who had walked into a screaming child's room to see a complete stranger standing over him, I don't know any actual martial arts, but I reckon I would have turned all ninja on them in such a scenario.

Just when you think life won't throw you any more surprises, she very cheerfully squealed my name… yes, my weird and unusual name.

"Minky!" she carefully closed the door behind her and raced over to give me a massive bear hug. My hands were still up in surrender, but with her embracing me, I managed to slightly relax and give her a light pat on the shoulders.

How this fancy woman had known my name was possibly one of the most unnerving things about the whole experience. I tried to look at her closely, but I was sure I didn't know her, not even from any of my Nan's soap operas. How did she know my name? Why was she treating me like a long lost friend?

She quickly turned her attention back to the child whose cry was now almost hysterical.

"Hush now Bobby," she said scooping the chubby baby into her arms and clutching him to her chest to soothe him. "I know you're a little frightened, but this is Minky, your grand-daughter." It was like she heard the hilarity in that statement because she gave a little chuckle. "It doesn't seem right does it?" she said giving me a cheeky wink and a smile.

I'm sure all the colour had drained from my face and my legs still felt like they were going to give way any moment. She either picked up on this or maybe it was the way I was still gaping at her like a guppie because she directed me to sit back down on the magical chair.

The baby had started to settle down a bit now it was in the safety of familiar arms, but he was still clutching her tight, and I knew there'd be no way he'd be happy to be put back down for some time.

"Minky, is this the first time you've used the chair?" She questioned me like we were fast and familiar friends. Nothing made sense, but I managed to give her a slow tentative nod. She gave me a very warm smile and sat herself and my baby sized Pop on a rocking chair I hadn't taken much notice of but was most likely used to feed the baby.

"We have so much catching up to do," but as if she'd remembered something she added, "you haven't really picked a great time for your first visit my friend, but I do have to say, I'm so happy to see you again."

I think I must have been wearing my 'have you gone cuckoo?' look, or maybe I was displaying a look of confusion, shock, fear or all of the above because her lovely friendly face was so warm and filled with genuine empathy for me.

"This *must* be the first time you've met me." She said putting some puzzle pieces together for herself. "Well it might be the first time you've met me, but it certainly isn't the first time I've met you." She smiled warmly. "I know quite a few things about the future too. By the time you are born, I will have already died so if it wasn't for this chair, we would have never met."

I was confused and scared. Was I in 1948? It certainly wasn't 2014. I was comforted by the fact she was so bubbly and friendly, but surely this was all a dream. I dug one of my fingernails into my palm and felt the sharp pain. Nope, it appeared somehow this wasn't a dream. It was definitely happening. What the hell?

"Isn't it funny to think how close we are? But then you don't know about any of that yet."

The more she talked, the more I felt there was a slight familiarity about her. It was her charismatic expressions when she talked that reminded me of Pop when he gets excitedly caught up in a story about one of his antiques. Even though she was chatting away like we were steadfast friends, I was positive I had never met her before in my life.

I really wanted to like her, but she wasn't making too much sense to me. My throat gave a weird kind of squeak as I cleared it to try and speak.

"I think I know where I am, but I am confused. Everything is different, and nothing is making sense." I croaked.

"Oh, you poor thing Minky, you don't look too well. I should properly introduce myself," she said, shifting the baby over to her other side to throw her right hand out to shake mine. "I'm Miranda, or Miz as you like to call me. I'm your great-grandmother, and if I'm not being too presumptuous, I believe I'm also your best friend."

SIX

"Let me try to explain." She paused for dramatic effect or maybe because I looked like I needed to take it all in a little bit slower. "We're not quite sure how, but this chair has some kind of time travelling ability. If you are holding something from a past time, it becomes, well, it's what you like to call a 'token'. If you are sitting in the chair holding the token and you are thinking about it's past, what the token did, or maybe the person or people who used it, it will instantly shoot you back to the time and place of when it was used. I guess the token is like a key to unlock that point in time, or maybe a ticket to something in the past. It's really quite incredible isn't it?"

"Incredible," I repeated still feeling dazed and perplexed. I looked down at both versions of the baby book that were now on the ground. "So a combination of that book and the chair is how I came to be here?"

"You're a smart sausage Minky, but then, *you* were the one who taught me about all this time travelling stuff, so I'm only relaying information you've given me." Miranda let out a little huff of air and said, "Even after many years of thinking about it, it still makes my head spin."

"So, that baby is my Pop?" I asked pointing to the child who had settled down now and was happy to be sitting on Miranda's lap but was still eyeing me cautiously. "And you're his mum and my great-grandmother?" I racked my brain trying to think of any details I could recall, anything Pop had mentioned about his mother.

Embarrassingly, there wasn't really that much I could remember about Pop's mum. Probably the only thing I knew was what she had already mentioned, she had passed away long before I was born. I was quite sure she was well loved and fondly remembered by those who had known her, but maybe because she'd never been in my life, any stories about her hadn't stuck with me. It was either the shock of everything that was going on, or my mind had turned to mush, but I felt I didn't know that much at all about the lady sitting next to me.

She seemed to understand this as her smile grew even wider and she said, "I have the feeling this is going to make you want to find out a bit more about me."

If I somehow managed to find my way back home perhaps I would want to do that, but at this point, I was really petrified and wanted to be back in the safety of my 2014 bedroom.

"Do you know how I can get back to where I came from?" I asked.

"You know, I still have so many questions about all this time traveling business, but your question is about the one thing I know I can answer.

"I'm pretty sure you need to hold the token you travelled here with, think about where you came from, and I'm guessing you then will just shoot right back to the exact moment you left." She paused. "At least, I think that's how it works. I've never actually done it myself, I've only seen you do it."

I had a million more questions running through my mind. "You said this isn't the first time we meet. Do you remember how we first meet in your time?"

"You sure catch on quick and ask great questions. You really are a smart girl Minky, I'm not surprised we're related.

"It is getting on a few years now, but I will never forget that day for so many reasons. I was about the same age you are now, p'rhaps slightly younger. You arrived out of the blue in my family home while I was listening to the wireless. No one else was there at the time. It was shall I say... a very interesting day."

We were interrupted then by the sound of a man's voice calling out for Miranda and heavy footsteps. It sounded like he was climbing the stairs from the shop and heading towards the room. For the first time since being there, I saw what I thought was fear in Miranda's gentle eyes. I had only just started feeling a little relaxed, and I had so many more questions for her, but by the look on her face, I sensed it wouldn't be a good idea to stick around for further introductions today.

"Minky, you have to get out of here now." She said scooping up the tattered older version of the little dog book and shoving it into my hands. "Remember, think of home and I promise, when the time is right, we will see each other again." There was no disguising the urgency of her wanting me out of there.

Being quite familiar with the house and the way everything sounds from that particular room, I knew those footsteps were now only seconds from the door.

I gave her the quickest goodbye and thanks with my eyes before I squeezed them closed and thought about the shop, the wildly wet rainy day and the musty, dark smelling corner of the shop I had not long ago left behind.

Although my eyes were closed, an incredibly strong flash of light lit up my eyelids, and a dizzy kind of sinking feeling came upon me.

SEVEN

In a snap, the movement stopped and I opened my eyes carefully. The chair and I were exactly where we had been as if none of what I had experienced had actually happened. I seemed so much more aware of everything, the smell, sights, I could hear Pop and his friend still bantering on the other side of the shop near the counter.

For about five solid seconds I sat there relieved to be back in the right place in time, but then it occurred to me how dangerous and unpredictable the chair was, and that this was definitely not a chair for relaxing and thinking in.

With fear it was going to send me hurtling somewhere unexpected in time again, I threw Pop's old baby book on the ground as if it was a hot potato and I shot out of the chair as fast as I could. I snapped my body around to look at the chair. There was still something quite alluring about it, and it was almost like it was cheekily smiling at me like it had shared its secret with me now and was daring me to continue on the adventure.

To be honest, the whole thing had scared the socks off me, and I wasn't sure I ever wanted to try using the chair again. My heart was still racing at a mile a minute, as I scrambled my way past the large items in the store to a safe distance away. I looked back towards the chair again and shivered. It was almost like there was a spotlight on it, and it was smiling proudly for revealing itself to me.

Even though it was so far up the back of the store, I decided I was going to have to cover the chair so I didn't risk having it give me that look anymore. I squeezed my way towards the front of the shop, where I was sure I had seen some white sheets under or near the counter. Bingo!

With Pop and Col still yarning about the weather or the football or whatever old guys chat about, I bravely but tentatively crept back, and when I was still at a safe distance but not too far away, I tossed the sheet like a fisherman casting out a net, and somehow managed to cover most of it so at least I didn't have to be so conscious of it looking back at me.

Without further hesitation I darted back upstairs to the safety of my bedroom, lay on my bed and put one of my favourite DVDs on to try and take my mind off of what had just happened.

I'd seen the movie a hundred times, but even though I was staring at the TV, I don't think I caught a word of it. I couldn't stop thinking about my weird experience.

I think I must have dozed off, and when I woke up the movie was over and my DVD was back to the title page with the characters faces flashing over the screen and a one-minute snippet of the title song playing over and over in an annoying loop.

The rain was still pretty persistent outside, but the thunder had subsided. I could make out the muffled sound of voices in the living area. It was definitely Nan and Pop, but their tones sounded different than usual.

Turning off the TV with the remote, I lay there for a minute, still trying to work out if what had happened with the whole chair thing had been real. My mind reasoned that there is no way it could have happened, it was all a dream and I probably haven't even left my bed today yet.

I studied my bedroom again, remembering how much more vivid the colours had been in the dream and the layout with the different old-fashioned furniture.

I stretched myself out of my comfy warm bed and headed into the living area where the voices were, and as soon as I entered, Nan and Pop fell awkwardly silent. Even though I was pretty sure it was now after lunch, I gave them a cheery "good morning," and then a giggle as I knew it was not morning, and the weather was making it anything but good.

Pop stood up from his chair at the dining table and hobbled off downstairs mumbling something about going for a drive.

"Is everything ok with you two?" I asked Nan after I'd heard Pop reach the bottom of the creaky stairs.

Nan let out a sigh, and lead me over to my chair at the dining table. "You've slept most of the day away Minky, you must be hungry, do you want something to eat?" Funny enough, I didn't realise I was hungry until she mentioned food, but the second she did, my stomach rumbled, clearly answering her question.

"Sounds great Nan, but is everything ok with you and Pop?" I asked again.

Nan busied herself in the kitchen, making a plate of leftovers for me so I could either chose to eat them as a plate or make up my own sandwich. Today there was leftover roast silverside, which I knew I would eat with salad on a fresh roll.

"Your pop found his old childhood books down in the shop." The second she said it, I felt sick for two reasons. Firstly, because I knew the chair incident was real and it wasn't a dream, secondly because I had totally forgotten to return his books after I had promised Nan I would.

Noticing Pop's old books piled neatly at the end of the dining table, I slumped my head heavily into my hands and I shook it slowly in disappointment with myself.

"I guess you could say he is pretty attached to some of his old things," Nan said pouring me a glass of my favourite cranberry juice.

I looked up at Nan with apologetic eyes.

"I am so sorry Nan, you even reminded me when I took them down, but I, well I don't really have an excuse." I could try and explain to her what had happened with the chair, but I still didn't really understand it myself. Plus I didn't think admitting to her "I forgot about them after I scared myself with a time travelling experience," would really cut it as a legitimate excuse.

"I hope I haven't caused problems with you guys." Although I'm first to admit I am not my mother's biggest fan, I still didn't like when my parents argued. It was a hundred times worse to see Nan and Pop fight, and knowing they were fighting about me was the worst feeling ever.

"Ah, your Pop will be fine, he'll get over it and really there was no harm done. I think it's a sore point for him because years ago, your mum and Aunty Cassandra were playing around with one of your great, great grand-fathers old pocket watches down in the store and someone came in and bought it. We had a young man, Jake working for us at the time and he didn't realise it wasn't for sale and with no price label he pretty much gave it away to a customer. Your pop was so mad as Jake couldn't remember any details about the buyer, it appears it has been lost for good. I am quite sure those old books don't have the same significance, but I guess there is sentimental value for him, and it has reminded him of that."

Nan was busying herself with cleaning up the table and doing the last of the lunch dishes. "Your mum was about your age at the time, and well, I'm sure you've heard adults talk about teenagers and how difficult they can be?" I nodded, even though I didn't really understand what the teenage fuss was all about. "He thinks you are going to be 'difficult' like your mum."

I'd just taken a reasonable mouthful of cranberry juice and almost spat it straight back out. I knew my mother was difficult, she was stubborn, very driven, high achiever with even higher expectations of others and herself. I wasn't sure how those things made for a difficult teenager.

"Will you excuse me, Nan?" I asked standing from the table, "thank you for a lovely lunch." Nan smiled. She seemed to be on my 'side' and hopefully, I could prove to both her and to Pop I was a 'better' teenager than my practically perfect (at least in her eyes) mother.

EIGHT

The following week at school, things were really starting to heat up. I had been impressed with the somewhat relaxed attitude my teachers seemed to have, especially with me starting part way through the year. But unfortunately, it seemed my gentle easing in period was well and truly over.

Unlike my old school, as I was only in year eight, I was only allowed to select one of my own subjects, which of course I chose physical education being my strongest subject. All other subjects were decided for me by the school, much to my disgust.

I've always known I'm not stupid, it's just my brain doesn't seem to work in an academic way. Maths confuses me, I have no memory for history and science... to me, science is like listening to aliens talk about the solar system.

I did somewhat enjoy my geography class, but that was probably only because Seshna was in it.

Seshna Prasad had a few months head start on me at Stone Park having only started there on the first day of the school year. She was the only child of two overachieving Indian parents who were both GPs.

If it could be possible, Seshna was even more of a sporty girl than I was. She was on both my hockey and netball teams and even though she was a pocket rocket who seemed to be everywhere at the same time, she never seemed puffed or even seemed to work up a sweat. Everyone commented about how much the netball team had improved since Seshna had joined. Our hockey team, which had apparently always had a good reputation, hadn't taken one loss this year with her on the pitch. Aside from the fact she was an amazing sportswoman, she was also a very cool chick.

"How frustrating was the weather this weekend?" I said to Seshna as we found our seats in the geography class.

"I know. I ended up going to the indoor rock climbing centre on Sunday. Mum gave me the idea when she said me moping around the house was driving her up the wall." We laughed but it was short-lived as the teacher stood in front of us and cleared his throat.

"Natural disasters." He said as he scrawled the words messily on the board. "The next unit we'll be studying is all about natural catastrophes occurring in the world. We'll look at whether they are getting worse and if there is evidence they can be prevented or impacts lessened." Seshna and I rolled our eyes and smiled at each other. Without a word we both knew it would be a unit, we would prefer to sleep through.

"You'll find it to be an intense unit with a lot to cover. Due to the fact natural disasters can cause great loss of life, it can be a some-what confronting subject, so please let me know if you need to talk or the subject makes you uncomfortable."

I made funny eyes at Sesh and she giggled.

"Sir," a voice came from behind us, "these girls are either making fun of you or the topic."

In disbelief at the hide of such a tattletale, I whipped my head around to face the guy who had spoken who was still rudely pointing at Seshna and I. I hadn't properly met him yet, but I knew our snitch's name was Cormack. I'd seen him in at least two of my classes so far, geography and maths, and he'd been quite vocal in both. There was nothing that particularly stood out to me about him except he seemed to be a bit of a teacher's pet and always looked a bit like he'd just been sucking on a lemon.

It shocked me a little that he'd thought our playful eye rolling and giggles were worth making such a big deal about.

"Thank you, Cormack." Mr Young walked over towards us and put a hand on each of our shoulders. "I have no doubt if these ladies are talking in class, they must already be experts on the topic and being talkers, they will excel at the final oral presentation all of you will give at the end of the unit." Everyone in the class except Cormack gave an audible groan. It seemed oral presentations were no ones favourite way to be assessed.

I tried my hardest to stay focused and take notes for the rest of the lesson, but I admit, I couldn't help but give my new arch nemesis Cormack a few dirty looks. He seemed almost pleased with my reaction and the attention I was giving him as if my disgust in him was his ultimate goal and he was winning. I resolved to do my best to ignore him, and not let him think he had gotten under my skin.

After class Seshna followed me to the cafeteria for the morning break.

"Can you believe that assignment? Presentations suck."

"I know, why do teachers think we want to do their job? I mean if we wanted to get up in front of a class and rattle on, we'd go to teacher school."

"Written assignments are so much better. You can get them over with and not have them hanging over your head for weeks." I hadn't thought of it like that. Written assignments to me hung over my head as heavily as oral ones as I usually left them until the last minute.

"What about that awful guy, Cormack?" I asked.

Seshna laughed. "You do realise your new 'boyfriend' is the other part of the Merrett twins?" I gasped in shock.

"No way! Cormack is Kayla's twin brother?" This revelation actually explained quite a lot.

Kayla Merrett was in our year, but pretty much seemed to think she ran the school. She was particularly possessive and rightly proud of the fact she was captain of every single one of the girls sporting teams. Naturally, she felt threatened by Seshna's abilities, and she had definitely been the most unwelcoming of all the girls when I had joined the teams too.

"So Cormack is the brains and Kayla is the brawn?"

"Sounds right, but don't let Kayla hear you saying that." Seshna giggled. "To top it off, their father is that judge who is always in the news because he tends to make unpopular decisions."

"Hmm, sounds like they are a bit of a controversial family who are not afraid of being unliked."

It was interesting to me that Kayla and Cormack were related and even shared a womb at the same time. I could make out the family resemblance now, both physically and behaviourally, except in many ways their gender went against the stereotype.

The rest of my day didn't improve on my difficult morning. I was given a research project to complete in science class, told we would have a big maths exam the following week. I was then issued with a new novel to study in English. Feeling overwhelmed seemed like a massive understatement.

I had an almost unheard of arrangement with my school as far as living in Sydney went. Nan and Pop's shop was only a handful of bus stops away from Stone Park so walking to and from school was actually very feasible and I preferred the walk rather than wait around for buses.

I had been avoiding contact with the chair now for days by not coming in the front door, but using the gate to the small backyard from the back alleyway. It meant I didn't have to walk through the shop at all, but it also meant Pop probably thought I was avoiding him. I truly wasn't, but I could tell he was still mad at me, so I felt like he would have been very happy not to be seeing me much.

"How was school Minky?" Nan asked setting a snack down in my spot at the table as I reached the top of the stairs.

"Overwhelming." Sitting down and devouring a slice of her delicious warm Madeira cake that had not long been pulled out of the oven. "I think my probationary period is over Nan, today I became a full-fledged Stone Park student with all the stress and drama that comes with it."

"You'll be right." She said scruffing my hair. "Everyone struggles, even your mum found school tough at times. Just take one thing at a time, you'll get through it." I nodded, but secretly felt way out of my depth and like I wanted to run away.

"I've actually got hockey practice in twenty minutes," I said getting up. "I'd better get changed and get back to the school." I loved my sport more than anything, but I seriously didn't know how I was going to be able to justify staying on the team if I wasn't able to keep up with my academic work.

I wasn't late, but I was the last girl to arrive at hockey practice. It was most likely only because none of the others lived close enough to go home and come back, so they would have changed in the bathrooms and launched straight into practice.

"Robinson, you'll have to pull your socks up if you want to stay on this team," Kayla said as I pulled on my shin guards and raced onto the pitch with my stick in hand. I was annoyed because I wasn't late, but it obviously looked like it with everyone already in full swing.

I joined the other girls with the drills without missing a beat and probably because of Nan's delicious carb-filled snack, I had more go than the energiser bunny.

We completely tore up the pitch with our running, weaving and ball practice. It felt really good to get through all the drills so efficiently.

To finish training we always ended with a practice penalty shootout where all the girls stand around the shooting circle and get a go at trying to shoot for goal. Our amazing goalkeeper Honora Sterling usually somehow manages to block each shot, so if you do get the ball past her, it is quite an achievement.

"Honora is sick today, so I need a volunteer to be goalkeeper for the shootout," Coach Klein said holding up the protective wear that all goalkeepers have to wear to shield themselves from the ball.

What was previously a group of excited and happy girls turned very quickly into a group of very quiet and sheepish ones. None of us wanted to look at Coach in the eye, so all eyes stayed glued to our cleats.

"Minky was the last to arrive, I think she should get the pleasure of goalie as a reward for her tardiness." Kayla piped up smugly.

My instant reaction was to throw her daggers with my eyes. It took everything inside me to stop myself from walking over and physically hurting her and screaming in her face that I WASN'T LATE! But at the same time, I didn't want her to think she had me rattled, so I took a deep breath, counted to three and tried to calm myself.

"There's no way I'll be as good as Honora at blocking shots, but I'll give it a go, sure," I said in my sweetest voice trying to exude confidence when the last thing I wanted to do was go and stand in front of the goal.

Seshna helped me put on the layers of protective gear, the body protector, leg guards, shorts, helmet, and gloves.

"You gonna be okay?"

"Yeah, I'll be fine. Getting hammered by the ball is probably the most appropriate way I can think to end this day."

"Those Merretts have really given it to you today haven't they?"

"I'm not going to let her think she's won. And there's no way I'm going to let her get a goal."

"Did you notice she brought her fan club?" Seshna said motioning to the stands discretely. Sure enough, Cormack was sitting on the stands with his head stuck in a thick textbook.

"Oh, fantastic," I said sarcastically through the masked helmet. I was now kitted up and ready to face the firing squad. It was usually my most favourite part of hockey practice, that is of course when Honora was standing in front of the goal doing the defending. I felt a lot more comfortable attacking as far as hockey positions went.

The other girls were already at the shooting circle, practicing firing the ball into the goal. The balls were shooting into the net at an intimidating speed.

I put on my bravest face, waddled awkwardly over to the goal and stood in front of the netted frame. Honora usually wore her own equipment she had bought to practices that fitted her well. The substitute goalie gear was not ideal as it had most likely been around since my mother had attended Stone Park and they had definitely seen better days.

I dropped my stick not once, but twice along the way. Not sure if it was from feeling a little daunted or because of the big bulky goalie gloves I wasn't used to.

It was a stupid thing to do, but I chose that moment to look up at the stands and notice Cormack who was now giving us his full attention, books away and everything.

The first girl took her shot and it easily sailed past me. I missed the next three before almost by accident blocking the fifth shot painfully with my thigh.

These girls definitely were not holding back. I felt tears sting my eyes from the whack of the ball on my leg. Even though I had a good layer of padding to protect me it still hurt.

Seshna gave me her shot and although I know she wasn't putting in her finest effort, the ball still sailed easily past me and was caught by the net.

I somehow managed to block three out of the next six shots, which I thought was pretty good for someone who wasn't used to being on the goal.

Kayla took her turn last. Looking at her eyes, I think we both felt like we had something to prove. I wasn't going to let her defeat me today and she was looking at me like she wanted to see me bloody and broken.

On top of everything, I could see Cormack's figure from the corner of my eye. It was extremely distracting and annoying. Even though I wanted to beat Kayla, I felt like I wanted to block her shot to get back at her snitchy brother Cormack more than anything.

Kayla drew her stick back and I braced myself, putting as much focus on the ball as I could. She swung with a lot of force and as if in slow motion, I threw my padded left arm up to block the corner she had aimed at.

I felt the ball brush my glove and heard the other girls gasp.

Unfortunately, I hadn't managed to stop the shot, the ball bounced off my glove and was hugged by the goal net.

Three of Kayla's loyal cronies cheered and clapped as though she had managed to score the winning goal at the Olympics.

Some of the other girls came and patted me on the back. I'm not sure if it was to thank me for taking on the job or more as a commiseration. Even though we were all on the same team, I'm sure they'd also like to see Kayla beaten occasion-ally.

I felt defeated, sore and tired as I helped Coach Klein pack up all the gear and walked my sorry-self home.

NINE

Before my parents had even settled me in to live with my grandparents and moved to Dubai, they had already purchased a ticket for me to visit them in the two-week mid-year winter break in July. I'd recently had my fourteenth birthday, a fairly low key dinner at home with Nan, Pop, Seshna and another friend Quinn. Nan had cooked up a feast and we'd watched DVDs in the lounge room all night and none of us slept a wink.

While I'd be in Dubai, Zac would be cele-brating his fourth birthday, so it seemed like a good opportunity for us to get together and my parents to see I could survive okay without them.

When they had promised me this visit, I wasn't keen to go at all, I was so sure it was going to be a ploy to get me over there and keep me there.

I had planned to try and find a way to get out of going before the trip came up, but by the time it came around I actually felt almost desperate to see my dad and brother and it was the perfect excuse to run away from the stresses of Stone Park.

To say I was now feeling inundated with school work was an understatement. It seemed like every second day we were given new assignments and I knew the work I was submitting was pretty sub-standard.

To be honest, even my beloved sports, which I had been prioritising over school work were not going well for me either. If Kayla wasn't part of the picture things would have been so much smoother, but for some reason, that girl had it out for me.

Unfortunately, the Dubai trip meant missing out on a netball camp in the second week of the school break. All the other netball girls on the team except Kayla thought I was crazy for wanting to go on an intensive netball camp over shopping in Dubai.

As captain of the first-grade year eight netball team, Kayla managed to use my absence from the camp as an excuse to kick me off the first-grade team and put me in the reserves. Even though I had protested, it had been half-hearted. With everything else mounting up, I didn't have the energy to fight to stay on.

Seshna had commiserated with me and said she thought she'd prefer to be on any team that didn't have Kayla on it and I was lucky to be on the team that had more fun. As Seshna was a key part of the winning formula, both of us knew she wouldn't have been allowed to leave the team even if she'd wanted to.

Pop's mood had been a bit brighter since his beloved football team had been on a bit of a winning streak, but things between us were still strained. He seemed to still avoid me where he could, and even though he did speak to me if I asked him a question, he never initiated any conversation with me.

An excuse to get away from school and the slight awkwardness at home seemed like it could be a welcome relief.

There were not many things I hated more than packing. I threw a pile of clean clothes in my suitcase and decided to take the novel we'd been assigned in English to read on the plane. It was meant to be a classic, but *The Slaughterhouse Five* sounded like a terrible book to me.

I hid my mid-year school reports down the bottom of the bag. I'd already skimmed over them and knew more than one of my teachers had mentioned I needed to focus more and to put in more effort to improve my grades. I would no doubt be forced to give up my sports and possibly get some tutoring help.

In the end, I didn't even read a word of my novel on the plane, choosing only to sleep and catch up on a few of the in-flight movies I'd been too busy at Stone Park to go to the cinema and watch.

Dad and Zac were waiting at the airport in the waiting zone when I had made my way through the customs and immigration area. The flight had been long and exhausting, and the first time I had ever flown anywhere without an adult. It hadn't helped that I had an annoying air hostess constantly checking on me as my in-flight guardian. As soon as I saw my Dad and brother though, my energy came flooding back.

"Did you bring your swimmers Minky?" Zac asked as we headed to the car. "We have a big pool at the complex, we go swimming every day don't we Dad?"

"Hang on a sec, are you sure you're only turning four Zac?" I asked giving Dad a smile. It felt like he'd been a baby when they'd left and now he sounded so grown up.

"I think both of you kids have grown exponentially in the last few months," Dad said.

"We're going to Wild Wadi Waterpark for my birthday."

"Sounds amazing Zac."

"And Dad, can we take Minky to the carousel at Marina Mall? It's not as big as the one back home, but you'll like it Minky 'cause it's really beautiful isn't it Dad?" I looked at my dad with a bemused look. My baby brother was talking a mile a minute.

"No merry-go-round in the world can compare to the one back home Zac," Dad said before he completely spoilt the mood by mentioning Jennifer. "Your mum was sorry she couldn't be here to pick you up Minky but unfortunately she has a big client that has been taking up a lot of her time. In fact, we haven't seen much of her for a good couple of weeks have we mate?"

"She'll be coming to Wadi though," Zac said, and I have to admit, I was so impressed and surprised at his confidence as he said it that I almost actually believed it.

I tried to picture the four of us frolicking at a water park together as a *real* family. I shook my head to snap myself out of the daydream. I'll believe that when I see it I thought.

Their villa was in a gorgeous complex not too far from all the action. They were occupying a two-story beautifully decorated home with four very generous bedrooms and five bathrooms. Again, I couldn't help to think of the contrast between the shophouse back in Newtown compared to the spacious villa.

My most favourite part of the house was the beautiful delicate lattice screens adorning the bottom halves of all the windows. I fell in love with them right away because I'd never seen anything like them.

It felt a little bit like a holiday house at a resort or somewhere quite tropical, but then the pretty lattice would catch my eye and I'd feel like an Arab princess in a mystical land.

The complex itself was exquisitely maintained by gardeners and maintenance men. All the families living in the complex were expats from mainly western countries. It seemed like a very friendly, lovely community. Staying here and escaping all the madness back in Sydney would suit me fine.

Dad, Zac and I spent the next two weeks enjoying the hot Dubai weather and going to every adventure park, playground and shopping centre we could, each one more grand and spectacular than the last.

Most nights, Dad would fire up the barbecue on the rooftop terrace and we'd have delicious meats and salads for dinner. Sometimes we had the neighbours join us and it was nice to put a face to some of the people Dad and Zac had been raving about to me on Skype.

I hardly saw my mother at all the whole time I was there. Not surprisingly to me, she didn't make it with us to the water park for Zac's birthday celebration. She said it would take up too much time and perhaps we could go out for a dinner to have another birthday treat before I left instead.

I wasn't going to hold my breath that it would happen, but amazingly on my very last night in Dubai, we all went out to dinner, all of us, including Jennifer.

"Oh wow Minky, you look gorgeous and so grown up," Jennifer said as I emerged from my room. I was a little shocked to see her there as she'd been so absent in my two weeks of visiting. I honestly thought there would end up being something to keep her from this final dinner opportunity. "Your Dad said you bought a lovely dress at The Dubai Mall."

I had fallen in love with the ditsy floral swing dress I'd picked up on our latest shopping trip and Dad said he'd get it for me as a belated birthday present. Without thinking I did a spin for her and she wolf-whistled back. I suddenly caught myself, forgetting I was mad at her and we didn't have a regular mother-daughter relationship.

"There is something missing though. A lovely dainty necklace would finish off your ensemble perfectly. Did you happen to bring the necklace I gave you?" she asked.

I sighed. No, I hadn't bought her tacky old necklace. I wasn't even sure where the silly old thing was.

On their last day in Australia, when they'd dropped me off and settled me in at Nan and Pops, just before the taxi arrived to take Jennifer, Dad and Zac to the airport Jennifer pulled me aside and presented me with a necklace.

Even though it was all a bit rushed, she'd tried to tell me how special it was to her, which I remember thinking everything she was blubbering about was a load of rubbish. I knew I'd seen the silly necklace in her jewellery box when I'd been snooping around the house back in Canberra, but I'd never in my life seen her wear it, so I knew it couldn't have been *that* special.

Jennifer had gushed about how my Dad had given it to her when they were dating and because it meant so much to her, she wanted me to have it so I'd feel connected to them.

It all sounded far-fetched to me, it seemed way more feasible that she had realised while packing that she should probably do something nice for the daughter she was abandoning, and instead of taking the time and making an effort to go out and buy something nice and new for me, she'd given me a piece of junk from her jewellery box, trying to pass it off as something thoughtful.

She hardly ever gave me the time of day, and now it felt like she was trying to be seen to be making an effort with me before she left. She would have done it publicly, but probably decided to wait until it was just the two of us so Dad didn't catch her out on a lie about where the necklace actually came from.

"I don't wear jewellery, Jennifer. You should know that." I noticed my comment and tone seemed to hurt her, but I had to make up for dropping my guard earlier.

"Look Minky, I'm so sorry I haven't been able to spend more time with you while you've been here." She said as if that was the only reason I was being so gruff with her as if it wasn't our usual way of communicating. It annoyed me greatly when she called me 'Honey' as if we had a normal mother-daughter relationship or some-thing.

"Well, it's nothing I'm not used to," I snapped.

"I honestly had good intentions this time, but I have this extremely demanding high profile client at the moment and…"

"Look, Jennifer, you don't have to explain or make excuses. I really don't care. Dad, Zac and I have had a great time together and Zac enjoyed his *actual* birthday with us which is all that matters."

Dad and Zac came darting down the stairs as though they were racing each other. Dad made appropriate comments about how nice his girls both looked tonight. Jennifer stopped making lame excuses for the rest of the night and stayed fairly quiet for her.

We went to an all-you-can-eat pizza restaurant where Zac was in heaven and didn't seem to notice the awkwardness between Jennifer and me.

To make matters worse Jennifer brought up the topic of my less than stellar report card and she started lecturing me about prioritising and how important school is.

Dad reasoned with her that it was still early days and I'd really only been there a couple of months, and thankfully Jennifer backed off a little or we could have started an international incident.

I hardly touched my pizza, I had a golf ball sized lump in my throat making it hard to eat and I felt miserable. It had pretty much been a perfect holiday up until tonight.

On the ride home, Dad began talking logistics on how he was going to get me to the airport and Zac to his school the next day. There was no talk or even any subtle signs my parents wanted me to stay with them in Dubai.

Anyway, I wasn't sure what would be worse, staying here with my mother, or going back to Sydney and facing a moody Pop, a chair that scared the wits out of me and my ever growing mountain of Stone Park demands. Who was I kidding? Sydney was definitely the lesser of two evils.

TEN

After visiting them and seeing where they lived, worked and played, I seemed to enjoy my weekly Skype calls with Dad even more. If anything, I now felt a slight pang of jealousy when he talked about people or things they'd seen or done, but at least didn't feel completely in the dark.

The most difficult thing with communicating with Dubai in real time is the time difference. It meant that to make time to talk and not be at work, school or sport, I had to wake at 6am and at the other end, Dad had to stay up until 11pm. Because of that, I didn't get to see much of Zac, and we all know what kind of impossible schedule Jennifer keeps so it wasn't hard to avoid contact with my mother. If anything cropped up between the weekly Skype calls, we'd text or email each other. Technology did make the world seem smaller.

I'd just finished dinner with Nan and Pop and knew I had a pile of homework I should have been doing. Pop had excused himself to go sit in front of the television. As the eating was done and Nan was taking the dishes to the sink, I pulled out the iPad mini to check my messages. I giggled as I read the email from Dad that included some funny photos of Zac and I that had been taken when we'd been at the aquarium.

"Dad says to say hi to you both." I said, "and he says he doesn't want any gloating from Pop about the game." I glanced over at Pop and although he didn't take his eyes off the TV I'm sure he heard me as the corners of his mouth curled up into a hint of a smile.

Dad's footy team, the Canberra Raiders, had gone down to Pop's team the South Sydney Rabbitohs 18-34 the previous weekend. Neither team had done very well in the last few years but Pop's team hadn't won a premiership in recent history. In fact, I think it had been more than forty years.

Dad's Canberra team wasn't a foundation club, but it had at least won a premiership more recently than the forty year drought Souths had suffered through. My Dad and Pop enjoyed digging each other about backing a losing team, but truth be told, I'm pretty sure both of them would have been happy to see each other's teams doing well.

"Nan, what team did you barrack for before you met Pop?"

"Oh no, I never had much to do with rugby league growing up. It wasn't until I met your Pop that I got into the rugby." She said as she wiped some of the dishes from dinner.

"I grew up in South Australia remember, and everyone followed the AFL, or VFL as it was called back then."

My Dad had been born and raised in Canberra, and Jennifer in Sydney. I'd never been to South Australia, which I guess you could say is more central Australia than the eastern states.

"Tell me about when you were growing up Nan. What were your parents like? Your friends? Family? Anything?"

Nan smiled and looked up dreamily.

"I had a wonderful childhood really. I lived in a very small town on a fruit block near the River Murray. We grew the juiciest, tastiest stone fruit you could ever imagine. It actually ruined me for life because I have never been able to find stone fruit that tastes as fresh or delicious ever since." I loved watching Nan talk about when she was younger. I could tell it really took her back to some good memories.

"Nan, what was school like for you? Did you struggle with juggling housework and home-work?" I said thinking of my own pile of homework in my bedroom I'd been successfully avoiding.

"I think I was very fortunate because my mum encouraged us to go to school, and also believed children should be children, and not have too much responsibility in the way of chores or housework." I smiled at her because this is how I felt living with her like she was letting me be a kid.

"My primary school was only a fifteen-minute walk up the road from our house, my cousin Audrey was my age and only lived two blocks down, and I would collect her and her little brother on the way to school." She still had a pensive look on her face as she recalled her younger years. "Most of the town was related in some way or another, my mum's brother even married my father's sister, which sounds weird, but it made Audrey and I cousins in two ways. I had other cousins my age in town too, but Audrey and I were the closest, we were inseparable."

Nan seemed to be enjoying reminiscing. "The high school was some distance away. It took us over an hour on the bus to get to the high school, but it never bothered us much because when Audrey and I were together, the trip never seemed too long."

It all sounded pretty good to me, eating fresh fruit picked straight off the trees, living and going to school with cousins and being related to half the town. I thought about my friends back in Canberra and those I'd met at Stone Park. I'd really never had a friendship with anyone as strong as Nan had with her cousin.

"Is the house and your family still there Nan?" I asked. "When did you last go back? What happened to Audrey?"

"Oh, it's been decades since I went back. Some of the family is still there, but all of my generation pretty much had to move out and away from the area, both for work and also to ensure we didn't marry our first cousins I guess." She said with a cheeky smile. "I am not complaining though, it was a wonderful way to grow up. Unfortunately, in the last few years, most of the fruit blocks have been sold off to big companies, some of them are no longer used for growing fruit but there are lots of vineyards around the area now. It's nothing like the good old days.

"I believe the family home is still there, although it doesn't belong to our family. The last time I went through it was still standing and it looked like they were taking pretty good care of it which is good because we had some great times there. Audrey got married and lives in Adelaide. We still talk on the phone at least once a month."

"So when did Pop come into the picture Nan?" I asked loud enough for Pop to hear from his recliner.

"Your Pop and I met when I came to Sydney to work. I had a job as a waitress and your Pop seemed to have an urge to try everything on our menu at the time. He came into the restaurant every day for over a month until he finally plucked up the courage to ask me out." She winked knowing it would encourage Pop to defend himself.

"It wasn't a month Leanne." Pop spoke up from his chair, fumbling with the remote control to work the mute button. "It was only two or three days, just enough time for me to work out if you were single. Plus, it was amusing for me to watch you at your job. I remember thinking you had a long way to go before you would be a first-rate waitress, you'd get all flustered and get the orders wrong. It was really more like cheap amusement for me." Pop said cheekily.

"But you've proved me wrong, and you've gone on to become the most incredible cook, mother, wife, and friend." Nan by his stage had walked over to Pop, given him a playful punch on the arm before wrapping her arms around his neck and giving him a quick peck on the cheek. "Well, you're certainly a lot more settled than my Mum ever was."

"Miranda certainly was something special," Nan said, which made my ears pricked up. I'd been trying so hard to avoid thinking or talking about the woman I had met in the chair incident. I thought I didn't want to know anything about her, but now her name had been brought up, I did start feeling a little intrigued.

"Can you tell me more about Miranda?" I asked leaving my iPad on the table and moving over to one of the empty lounge chairs.

"Mum was always so different to all the other mothers I knew. It was almost like she lived decades before her time. Like she had an insight into the future or something." I gulped, trying to hide my knowledge that she most definitely *did* know something about the future.

I looked around at all the pictures in frames around the living area, "So, is she in any of these photos?" I asked.

"Oh, I'm sure she is." Said Nan, walking over to a hutch, picking up a slightly dusty old frame to bring over to me. "This one here is Miranda's wedding photo. She was a stunning bride wasn't she?"

I examined the photo and had to agree. The picture was an aged sepia colour. Even though there wasn't really any colour in the photo, there was still plenty of detail. I noticed the gorgeous large princess style wedding dress, I could make out she was wearing delicate drop earrings and a necklace but what really caught my eye was front and centre in the photo she was holding the biggest bouquet of flowers I think I've ever seen a bride carry in my life. I examined her face, and sure enough, it was without a doubt the same woman who I had talked with in my room, with my baby sized Pop in her arms.

Possibly the most interesting thing about her was that unlike the man standing next to her in a military uniform with a straight back and sombre face, Miranda wore the most dazzling smile you could imagine.

"She's smiling," I said, stating the obvious, but both Nan and Pop seemed to get what I was saying.

"Yes, she broke all the rules for her time Mum did. She was never going to allow anyone to tell her what she could and couldn't do. If she wanted to smile in a photo she would." Nan and Pop gave each other a knowing look and Nan walked over to another shelf, plucking another smaller framed picture and handed it to me.

This one appeared to be much later in her life but it was still a photo that had been around a lot longer than I had. She looked in the second photo to be somewhere in her fifties or sixties, I'd say younger than my Nan was now but still with a good few years behind her.

The photo was in colour, and judging by other photos I had seen that looked about the same era, I guessed it had been taken sometime in the 1980s. It was a little yellowed but I could make out in the background the iconic Taj Mahal. Although the photo had been taken from a distance, I could still make out it was Miranda. She was smiling broadly, and on her body, she was wearing a beautiful bright Indian sari.

"She went to India?" I asked amazed.

"Oh yes, your great-grandmother travelled all over the world before she died, which wasn't something many people her age did back then. Especially not single women travelling alone. She brought things back from all her travels, but the best things she brought back with her were her stories. She could tell a story better than anyone I'd ever met and managed to find herself in her fair share of interesting situations." I smiled as I thought about Miranda the adventurer travelling all over the world, meeting people and starring in her own stories.

"And the shop, Pop? She lived here too, didn't she?" I asked.

"She did. Mum actually bought this shop and home, set it up from scratch and then started running the shop while Dad was away fighting in the war. It was quite unheard of in that day and age for a young woman to be so entrepreneurial, and to make such decisions without a man. Even though she was modern before her time, she also had a respect for old things and for history. I know she's the reason I am so obsessed with antiques and could never give up the shop."

"What was your Dad like Pop? I don't even think I know his name." I quizzed, anticipating another candid response. Pop shifted in his chair and his cheerfulness left.

"My Dad's name was James. I guess you could say he and Mum were chalk and cheese to start with, but when he went away to fight in the war it changed him. Everyone said he came back a totally different person, but they didn't have me until he returned so I can't really comment on that." Pop said with a sombre face and tone, making me think I should stop questioning him about his father.

I thought of the chair downstairs and how nice it would be to see Miranda again. I wondered if I could figure out what 'token' I would need to go back to see her? She had given me a clue that we'd previously met when she lived in her old family home and she was about my age.

"Pop, do you know where your mum lived when she was a girl?"

"She lived in a lovely old modest weatherboard house with a white picket fence very close to Waverley Park in Bondi. I remember she occasionally used to drive me past and point it out to me when I was a kid."

"Could you drive me past so I can have a look one day Pop?"

"Sorry, unfortunately not. They demolished it years ago, way before you were born Minky. The whole area is a sea of apartments buildings now." I slumped a little to think that all the history was now gone.

"Do you think you might have anything your mum might have owned when she was a girl?"

He gave a bemused snort. "Look around Minky, I'm sure we do."

"What do you think was your Mums favourite item?" I asked. "Was there anything she found particularly special? Did she leave you anything that she said never to sell or get rid of?"

"Well, she was never too precious about anything much. I don't know if there was ever any one thing she liked or wanted to keep. Although she did tell me quite often to make sure I do hold on to some of the family things, as they are part of our family history, and part of our family future. Thankfully though I do get pretty attached to our old things."

All three of us looked around the living room we were sitting in that was filled to overflowing with items from the past, a collection impressive enough to take on the likes of the jam-packed shop below us. All three of us burst into laughter.

It felt very good to have a good laugh again. It also seemed like Pop had forgiven me for the book incident, and his forgiveness felt pretty good too.

ELEVEN

The conversation with Pop about his mum had been excellent for our relationship, and much to my nan's delight, Pop and I seemed to be getting on better than ever.

Every day after dinner we would spend a bit of time talking about the old days and I'd quiz them about some of the items around the house making sure I didn't take them anywhere near the stairs to the shop.

Miranda often became the main topic of conversation, and the more I heard about her, the more I found myself itching to travel back again to see her.

Pop told me all about the history of the shop and the apartment upstairs, how the toilet used to be outside, and they had extended and added the toilet inside in the 1980s after Nan and Pop had taken over and they started having kids of their own. I think it brought me an unhealthy level of pleasure to think there was a time in her life when my precious mother would have had to use an outside toilet. It's the sort of thing she would never have admitted to.

Probably the thing most upsetting to me was my poor Pop didn't have many nice memories of his dad at all. Pop had been born about a year after his dad had returned injured from the war.

James had been injured in battle and had found it difficult to get employment with both his mental and physical war wounds. Miranda had tried earnestly to get her husband interested in taking over duties in the shop, and back to his pre-war self. Unfortunately, though he had started drinking heavily, and when Pop was still quite young, his father had died unexpectedly in an accident no one seemed to want to tell me anything about.

It took a lot of prodding, but Pop finally told me how Miranda had died. Maybe he thought I was too young to hear about it. I have to admit the details of her death were horrible. But I wasn't a baby, and I watch the occasional news story, so I know bad and tragic things happen all the time. I'd been taking Mr Young's geography class in natural disasters so I was no stranger now to sad events where lots of people die.

The story I was told was that Miranda had a taste for adventure. Just before Jennifer, her first grandchild was born in 1974, at the age of only forty-nine Miranda decided to retire early and left her shop and house to her only son and his new wife. She then spent several years travelling the world and having amazing adventures everywhere she went.

She was in Puerto Rico in 1986 when she had tragically been caught in a hotel fire which had been set by an arsonist. Almost one hundred people had perished and countless more were injured in what was then known as the Dupont Plaza Hotel. Most of the fire victims had been in the casino area downstairs and not in their rooms when they died. All of Miranda's belongings were undamaged and still upstairs in her hotel room however she was nowhere to be seen. The Puerto Rican authorities had eventually returned her things to the family, but unfortunately, her body was never identified or returned to Australia to be laid to rest.

This all happened when Jennifer was twelve years old, so Miranda died a long time before I was born. It made me feel sick to think that Miranda's exciting life was so needlessly cut short at only sixty-one years of age.

After learning so much about how she had been treated by her abusive husband and the tragic details of her death, I was more determined than ever to travel back to see Miranda again. There were so many things I needed to warn her about. I didn't know how I was going to get back, but I knew I had to try so I could perhaps prevent some of the terrible things from happening to her.

TWELVE

I had started using the front door to the shop again and was even glancing towards the chair as I walked through the shop. It was definitely luring me back to it. I'd decided to ask Pop what he knew about the chair and where it came from.

He normally kept an old radio playing softly near the counter, I'm not sure how many times I had heard him say "Radio is a TV for people with imagination," and that "it keeps an old man company." But on this day, rather than the radio, he had dusted off a charming gramophone and was playing a beautiful scratchy old upbeat record that almost made me feel like we had stepped back in time… without the help of the chair.

I dumped my school bag near the counter and approached the box with the decorative protruding horn. My fingers instinctively went to turn the handle.

"Ah-ah, no need Darl, I've just cranked it. It'll be right to play on for a while now." Pop said stopping me in my tracks.

"The sound is amazing Pop." The jazzy vibe of the big band tune had a tone so different to anything I had ever heard before in real life.

"You won't hear quality sound like this on those pod things you put in your ears." I smiled half because he was probably right, but also because it was comforting to have him bag out technology and criticise new things. "How was school today?"

"Yeah, okay," I said casually not wanting to remember the terrible day I'd had or give any hint of trouble to Pop. Both Kayla and Cormack had been making my Stone Park days slightly miserable. When I didn't have either of them in a class it was decidedly bearable. Unfortunately, I always had at least one or two classes a day with one or the other Merrett twin.

"I've been meaning to ask you about a chair I found up towards the back corner of the shop a few weeks ago," I said nodding towards the direction of the chair and wondering how much I would need to describe it for Pop to know which chair I was talking about. I needn't have worried because I could tell he knew which chair I was talking about straight away.

"You know, I'd forgotten all about that ratty old chair. People always think this shop is a great big mass of unorganised junk, but it's not true. I know every item I have in here, and about where they're from and often who's owned them. That sort of detail is valuable to a collector." Pop continued pottering around. "The only thing I don't seem to know anything about in this shop is the silly old chair." I slumped a little, unable to hide my disappointment.

"I have no idea where the ugly thing came from. One day, I came in and it was just sitting right here, dumped in the middle of the shop." He pointed to a spot near the counter.

"Are you kidding? Someone brought it in and left it in the shop without asking if you wanted it or even hanging around to find out?" I asked.

"I imagine someone thought it looked old and perhaps, being an antique store, we would want to sell it." He shook his head, "We're not an op shop, you don't just dump your second-hand junk and run."

"How long ago did it appear?"

"Hmm, not that long ago really, maybe six or seven months ago. Actually, I'd say it was about the same time you arrived to live with us Minky. I was going to take it straight to the skip, but then I thought it might be someone's cup of tea, so I dragged it out of the way, up to the back corner of the shop."

If Pop's memory was right, it gave me the shivers to think the chair had appeared around the same time I had moved into the shop with them. What if the chair had appeared specifically for me? Maybe the reason I was gravitating to it was that it was meant to be there for me to use it.

I decided I needed to take another close look at the mystery chair.

The next weekend I woke up early, pulled on my jeans and a T-shirt and raced downstairs before I lost my nerve. I approached the chair, and slowly removed the sheet I'd thrown over it.

Yes, it was old and tattered, but I don't think I'd put it in the ugly category Pop had placed it in. There was definitely a charm about it, that is if I could look past the fact it still scared me senseless.

Making sure I didn't have anything in my hands resembling a 'token' which could accidentally shoot me off to goodness knows where. I carefully sat myself down on it. The leather upholstery had certainly seen better days.

I let my right-hand travel down cautiously between the armrest and the seat cushion and to my surprise, I touched something cool and metallic. I carefully pulled out the foreign object only to find it wasn't something foreign to me at all. It was, without a doubt, my mother's precious necklace. The one she had given me just before they'd moved to Dubai.

Even though I had told my mother it meant nothing to me and I didn't wear jewellery, this was really all a big lie as I honestly thought it was a very pretty and unique necklace. I particularly loved the fact every time I had worn it, I'd received lots of nice comments about it and people always wanting to know where I'd gotten it.

The main reason I didn't wear it all the time was because we were not allowed to wear jewellery to school. It really had nothing to do with not liking it. I actually couldn't remember seeing it for a while.

I inspected the chain and pendant in my hands and noticed it was looking very tarnished. It obviously hadn't liked being down the side of the chair in the musty old shop for the last few months. I must have been wearing it the day I met Miranda I thought. I racked my brain to try and remember what I'd been wearing when I'd met her. I could picture what Miranda and little baby Pop were wearing, but I couldn't recall my clothes when I thought of it.

I shoved the necklace in my jeans pocket, grateful to have lost it in the chair and not somewhere where it may never have been found again.

Wondering what other treasures could be hiding in the chair I picked up the heavy seat cushion. Nothing. I inspected the rest of the chair, looking for hidden buttons or contraptions or something that could possibly explain what had happened before, or how the chair had special powers. There was nothing to suggest it wasn't just an ordinary old chair.

Nan called out to me from upstairs wondering if I was going to eat breakfast before I went to my netball game. I had completely forgotten I had a game that day.

I dashed upstairs and changed into my netball uniform, grabbing a yoghurt and muesli bar to eat on the way to the game. Further chair inspections were going to have to wait.

Thirteen

Pop's footy team thrashed the Manly Sea Eagles, another Sydney rugby team, 23-4 and I ended up having an equally satisfying win in my netball game the same weekend. To my shock, I was awarded player of the match for the first time ever.

It wasn't until the next day when Nan was about to start cooking something for dinner when Pop suggested instead perhaps we could all go out to dinner to celebrate our wonderful sporting successes from the weekend and give Nan a break from the kitchen.

"How 'bout we go to Riccardo's for dinner?" Pop said, "I'll even get the Chevy out so we can travel in style." Nan and I nodded excitedly. We didn't need to be asked twice about dining at the restaurant, which was by far our family's most favourite place to eat out. I raced to my room to get out of my netball uniform and into something suitable for dinner.

I decided to wear the pretty dress Dad bought me, but because it was still winter and a lot cooler in Sydney than it had been in Dubai, I wore a mauve long sleeve cardigan over the top of it with some white tights underneath.

I twisted my hair up off my neck, pinched my cheeks to give them a rosy glow (something I'd seen Nan do) and smoothed some clear lip gloss on my lips.

Then I noticed the necklace Jennifer had given me, hanging on the edge of my dressing table mirror. It would look perfect with the dress I thought, noticing Nan must have found the blackened necklace in my jeans pocket and worked her magic on it, rubbing all the tarnish off. It now looked super sparkly and as good as new.

"You're one awesome lady Nan," I said out loud, even though there was no way she would have heard me.

I heard the horn honk out front and Nan sang out to me to see if I was ready. I raced out to meet her in the kitchen.

"Minky, sweetheart," Nan said wiping away a tear, "you're really starting to resemble your mum." Hmm, thanks Nan, I thought, not what I was hoping to hear, but I didn't let Nan see me rolling my eyes at her comment.

Pop had his pride and joy running out the front. His immaculate old sea-mist green Chevrolet convertible. Excitedly I jumped in the back while Nan locked up the shop.

"How did I get so lucky to get a date with the two best looking sheilas in Sydney?" Pop asked as I clicked my seatbelt in and Nan did the same in the front.

Dinner was incredible. I had a beautifully rich flavoured pasta dish from the specials menu, Nan had her favourite, veal parmigiana. Pop ate a whole large pizza with the lot all to himself. Afterward, I enjoyed a generous portion of tiramisu while Nan had an espresso, and Pop finished his meal off with some limoncello as a digestif.

Although the food is divine, the best part of Riccardo's by far is the view. It is right on the water at Double Bay, overlooking Sydney Harbour. It was always busy, but it felt like only the locals seemed to know it was there because it was so well tucked away. I couldn't help think of how blessed I was to be living in such a pretty place.

"How about we go somewhere and find an ice cream?" Pop asked.

"Yes please!" I said excitedly.

"Bob! Minky has just eaten a great big creamy tiramisu."

"Ah, she's young... And by all accounts and awards, if she can play a game netball that hard, she can surely work off a few extra calories." I gave Pop a big smile and gabbed Nan's hands.

"Please Nan?" I begged.

"Ok, my arm is twisted." Nan surrendered.

Pop took care of the bill and had a quick but animated conversation with the actual Riccardo on the way out.

We piled back into the Chevy and went for a drive, getting sneak peeks of the water every now and then. It was such a mild night, even for winter and there were quite a few people out for a Sunday night.

It was so much fun riding in a charming old car with the top down. I couldn't help appreciate the top down thing would never happen on a winters night in Canberra. It's way too cold there in winter.

Pop easily found a great car park right on a street near Bondi Beach, which surprised both Nan and me, as Pop was constantly complaining about what a tourist trap Bondi had turned into and how bad parking was now. We jumped out of the car and walked past the old Bondi Pavilion towards the famous beach and shops.

Pop gave me ten dollars and said I could grab myself a treat. He and Nan had found a spot to watch both the people and the waves. They both insisted they didn't want an ice cream and I should just look after myself.

I headed over to a small ice cream shop I'd never noticed before. Although I'd really only been to Bondi a handful of times, I was pretty sure I hadn't seen it at any other time. I guess like most places and it seemed especially in Sydney, there were always new stores popping up where old ones close. I'm sure it is Pop's greatest fear about his own shop, that it will be closed down and replaced with a new chain store or something.

Although it only had a tiny frontage, the line for the ice cream shop was quite long, however, that seemed like a good sign to me. By the look of the generous and delicious looking servings, I could see why it was a popular spot. Even with a large queue, it didn't take long to get to the front of the line so I thought they must be good at both ice cream and customer service.

After drooling over the delicious choices, I ordered a half cookies and cream and half salted caramel cone from a pimply teenage guy and paid.

"Here, take a cone each for your Mum and Dad," an older lady said from behind the counter and before I could decline she had thrust a cardboard tray with two more cones in it into my hands and nodded her head towards Nan and Pop.

"Oh, they're not my parents, they are my grandparents and they didn't give me enough money for all of this," I said shaking my head to refuse the generous ice cream cones she was offering.

"I insist," the lady said with a twinkle in her eyes and a quick wink before returning to the long line of customers.

"Well, thank you very much," I called after her, but she was already back serving customers in the busy store. The lady had felt slightly familiar to me, but it was probably because she'd obviously mistaken me for someone else and was being so friendly.

I balanced all the ice cream cones over to Nan and Pop who were surprised when I showed them their treats.

"The lady at the little ice cream shop insisted," I said giving Pop the change and presenting them with the tray of ice creams under their noses so they couldn't resist.

"Well, this one has my name all over it," Nan said picking up the orange and pink cone with creamy looking jaffa and strawberry ice cream. "My two favourite flavours!"

"How did you know I can't say no to rum and raisin Minky?" Pop asked grabbing his cone.

"Honest Pop, it was a complete fluke, I didn't even order them, they were a gift."

We decided to wander up the beach back towards the car as we devoured our delicious ice creams. I noticed Nan and Pop held each other's hands which I thought was pretty cute for a couple in their mid-sixties.

There was a very light fresh breeze, but it wasn't freezing cold for a winter night. Life was actually pretty good I thought.

If I'd been thinking about the big geography presentation I had the next day, I wouldn't have been feeling so relaxed and carefree. I hadn't even decided what I was going to talk about, let alone started any work on it yet.

Fourteen

I lay in my bed, eyes wide open and unable to get back to sleep. Everything about yesterday had been so wonderful, even down to eating the most delicious ice creams any of us had ever tasted.

I'd been so exhausted from all the excitement of the weekend and probably also from a tummy full of food, that when we'd arrived home from Bondi, I'd changed into a long sleeved nightie and snuggled under my covers I'd fallen asleep really easily. I'd even slept for a few hours, but I now found myself wide awake in the middle of the night, listening to the odd creaks and squeaks of the old house. Living on a busy main street, there was not normally complete silence outside, but it was pretty quiet tonight.

There were a million thoughts going through my mind, most of them about the chair, and also Miranda. I couldn't stop thinking, that if I could go back to see her before she made some big mistakes, like marrying her abusive husband, and being in that particular hotel when the fire happened, perhaps she would be alive to see me born, or even better still be alive today.

It seemed like such a long time since I had used the chair and time travelled, but certain parts of the memory were still vivid in my mind. Instead of the fear I had felt straight after the event, my memory of the time travel now a few months had passed, were less of the fear and more of the excitement and good stuff. I had started almost longing to go back and I knew next time, I would have more confidence and would definitely be more prepared for it.

I racked my brain trying to recall what Miranda said she'd been doing when she'd seen me travel before. Was she home alone watching TV? No, it wasn't TV, she said listening to the 'wireless'.

I picked up my phone and Googled 'what is a wireless', and quickly discovered it is basically an old-fashioned term for a radio? Radio!

The image of an old wooden radio on the shelf in the dining room popped into my mind. I was positive it had to have been Miranda's.

I looked at my iPad dock at the side of my bed. '4:23am' glowed out in soft yellow neon. Still more than an hour and a half before Nan and Pop would start rousing.

I pondered my dilemma. If I get caught with Pop's old family radio in the shop like I did with his childhood books, there would be hell to pay, but then, if I do it at this time of night, I would probably have more chance of getting away with it. Now I knew a bit more about what I was doing, I would absolutely make sure the radio got back to its place on the shelf.

My reasoning and self-psyching continued for some time because it wasn't until my clock read '5:41am' that I snuck out of my warm bed. By then, I had been listening to the silence of the house broken only by Pop's rhythmic snoring. I'd been psyching myself up and thinking about what I was going to do for so long, once I'd made the decision to go for it, it felt like I sprang out of bed and leapt straight into action.

I trod lightly past my grandparent's room and into the living area. The floor tiles so cold almost felt like they were burning my bare feet.

Standing on tiptoes I reached up to grab the radio on the shelf near the dining table, which to my surprise had a power cord attached to it. I hadn't really thought about how it may have been operated, I was really only expecting the box, so the cord, which wasn't in my mental planning, was nearly my undoing.

As I pulled the box towards myself the cord almost brought down a china teapot and a picture frame. Somehow in the dim light, I was able to keep everything reasonably quiet and unbroken. I froze and listened to whether I could hear Pop's snores from the end bedroom and didn't move until I did.

I sighed heavily and resolved to move more carefully and slowly. I coiled the cord up in my left hand to keep it from dragging along the floor.

There were a few loud squeaky stairs that were not so noticeable during the noise of the day, but I was able to carefully avoid them all and inch my way downstairs to the shop without making a sound.

I'd never done much sneaking around the shop in the middle of the night, so it surprised me that there was enough light for me to see how to move around. Being the middle of the night and so still though, it felt just as spooky as it had the previous travelling day, even without the thunder and lightning show. I was kicking myself for again not thinking about bringing a torch or something to help light the way again. Honestly, would I ever learn?

Finding the chair I sat myself down in it, closed my eyes and tightly clung to the radio thinking about Miranda. It almost felt as if the chair said "finally!" and in a flash that familiar flood of light and moving feeling came back. I was travelling again.

FIFTEEN

When I opened my eyes I was definitely no longer in the shop or even the shophouse. It was somewhere I knew I hadn't been before, and I was positive I was no longer in the 21st century anymore.

The first thing I noticed was the sound of the voices on the radio. They came through with a kind of tinny sound, and nothing like the clear digital sound we have today. There was a lot of expression in their voices though, like they were reading out a play.

The second thing I noticed was what I was wearing. Not only was I not wearing any shoes, but I also hadn't thought to change into proper clothes, so I was still wearing my nightie, which to my embarrassment had the faces of all five 'One Direction' boys on it. It felt as if I was sitting there almost naked.

Feeling extremely vulnerable and inadequately clothed, I noticed the young girl, who I desperately hoped was Miranda so I could get away with my embarrassing wardrobe issue.

The poor girl had been splayed out on her tummy, on the longest lounge chair in the room. When she'd seen me, she had sat up and curled herself into a small ball, her arms holding her lanky legs to her chest. She looked now exactly how I had felt the first time I had travelled. Her eyes couldn't hide her terror and there was not one scrap of colour left in her face.

"Are you Miranda?" I somehow managed to ask, and when I noticed her eyes widen and jaw drop even lower, I knew I had my girl. I had to pull myself together because I knew this time it was going to be up to me to explain things.

"Hi. My name is Minky," I said standing up, placing the radio down carefully on the chair, straightening my nightie to make sure it was covering me adequately. I stuck my hand out confidently for Miranda to shake. Very hesitantly she did. "This is going to sound very weird, but I'm here from the future."

Miranda's head slowly nodded, but her face was near white and she still looked like she was seeing a ghost.

"Well, I guess, that kind of makes sense," Miranda said slightly relaxing her posture. I knew instantly this kid was born cool.

Miranda was wearing a flimsy light blue cotton dress and like me had no shoes on her feet either. She had curly blond hair in a bob just above her shoulders with a couple of bobby pins holding it away from her eyes. Unlike the last time I had met her, her hair was quite unruly and unkempt.

Miranda seemed very interested in what I was wearing as well, and was staring at the faces and words splashed across my nightie.

"I've never seen a dress with faces on it like you're wearing. It's so bright and colourful." She looked quite mesmerized. "Who are they? What's 1D?"

"Um, I'm a closet OneDirectioner," I said under my breath. Of course, I knew she wouldn't know what that meant so I tried to explain, "These guys are my secret boy-friends." Miranda still looked confused.

"If you want to keep them a secret why do you have their faces so brightly displayed across your clothes? And does everyone in the future wear outfits like you?"

I shouldn't be cracking jokes, not when I was meant to be explaining what was going on. I resolved to try my best to answer everything honestly and simply but at the same time try not to make it confusing for poor Miranda. It did quickly cross my mind how funny the future would be if everyone - men, women, and children wore character nightwear as their day clothes!

"No, this is what I wear to bed, so only my family know I like these guys. Not all, but I guess some clothes in the future do look a bit like this," I said holding it out in front of me, "but this is a nightie probably very similar to what half the girls my age wear in my time."

I looked around the room. After living at the shophouse for so long I was pretty used to old things, but these old things were all pretty new.

Although it wasn't a large room, it possibly seemed larger than it was because there wasn't a whole lot of furniture in it. In fact, there wasn't that much in it at all, unlike the shophouse which is full of knick-knacks and dust collectors.

Aside from the one radio - or wireless - it also wasn't scattered with modern conveniences and electrical devices, and probably the most stand out thing to me was that it was extremely neat.

The thought came to me that someone else could walk in and catch me in my sleepwear.

"Is there anyone else here with you Miranda?" I asked. She looked a little bit awkward like she shouldn't be admitting to a stranger she was home alone, and some of the pink returned to her cheeks.

"Mum has gone up to Newcastle to help look after her sick aunt and my Dad was given tickets to the Empire Games so he took my brother for the day." Then she quickly added, "But Mrs Frank next door is keeping an eye on me though, and she will come over and check on me soon if she doesn't hear from me."

"Ah, so, that's why you were listening to the wireless." I thought out loud. "Pop always says, radio is the TV for people with imagination. It's like the olden day version of spending a day in front of the telly."

"What's the telly?" I looked around the room, noticing another reason the room looked unusual. There was no TV, and the lounge chairs were arranged to face each other, not to face the big black box they sit around today.

"The TV," I said to a continued blank look. "Television?" Still nothing. "Ah, you'll find out about it in the future."

"How far into the future are you from?"

"Well, what year is this?" I asked as if I could rattle off mathematics in my head, which I so couldn't do.

"Nineteen thirty-eight," she said and I tried to do the calculations using my fingers, but I failed miserably.

"Let's see, it's the year 2014 in my time," I said out loud still tapping away at my fingers. I was hopeless at maths.

"What? That's seventy-six years away" Miranda said, doing the calculations super fast in her head. I was really impressed as there were no calculators or iPhones in sight. "I was born in 1925 so it means I'd be eighty-nine years old in your time… Wow, I'm nearly ninety," she said in awe.

I've never played poker in my life, but my dad had often said over the years I couldn't keep a poker face if I tried. I must have been looking pretty forlorn as I tried to figure out if now was the best time to tell her she doesn't make it to 2014. This must have been obvious to Miranda.

"Well, obviously I don't live that long. I mean, who lives to age ninety anyway? Not many people I know. Oh please don't look so sad," she said trying to comfort me because my face was obviously unable to hide what I was thinking. "How about you just tell me how you got here?"

Knowing how scared I'd been during and indeed after my first "travelling" experience, I was amazed at how incredibly accepting and calm Miranda was. I gave her the rundown on the chair, how it worked right up to how I'd only just figured out how to visit Miranda for the second time. I also told her about the shop, the house, and that we are related. She sat for some time taking it all in.

"Hang on, I buy a shop? In Newtown? Home of the Bluebags?" She asked with disbelief. I honestly thought she would have been more amazed that her great-grandchild was standing there in front of her, one year older than she was.

"I'm not sure what the Bluebags are, but yes, you did buy a shop, and it's still in the family."

"The Bluebags are a football team, but they're nothing on our team South Sydney District. We haven't won a premiership for a couple of years now, but we are still the best team in the league."

I couldn't help but smile. I had forgotten Pop's unhealthy obsession with the South Sydney Rabbitohs rugby league team had stemmed from his mum Miranda, who it seemed had been loyal to the team apparently since she was a child.

"We were runners-up last year, so I think we'll get there this year." Of course, I didn't know the footy results for 1938 off the top of my head, but I did know they had not had a great run for decades in 2014. I certainly didn't want to give away that their glory days were well and truly a thing of the past. I feel like I was able to keep a pretty good poker face about that.

"I wouldn't worry too much about the Bluebags, I haven't even heard of that team. I think you should concentrate on the fact you become a successful business owner. It's a great feat for anyone, even in 2014." Miranda seemed to agree.

"I think Mrs Frank would let me leave the house if I have a friend to go around with. Do you want to get out of the house?"

I looked down at my naked feet and embarrassing attire ready to decline the offer.

"Don't worry, you can borrow something of mine to wear." she laughed. I didn't need to be asked twice.

"Well, in that case, you bet."

I followed Miranda into her bedroom, which was quite meagrely decorated and obviously shared with her brother. I couldn't remember when the great depression was, but it reminded me things could have been pretty tough for them and in comparison I realised I never really missed out on anything. Still, they had a nice house which was probably better than some people.

Even though I was only about a year older than Miranda, I was quite a bit bigger in size. I wondered if it had anything to do with the hormones they say are in chicken? I always thought it was an urban myth, but I could remember them going on about stuff like that in the news, I'd never really paid much attention.

Miranda didn't mention my size, but she gave me a lovely yellow dress to try on. It looked like a hand-me-down she hadn't quite grown into yet. It fit me like a glove.

Miranda also changed into a cute pink summer dress, and we both put on a pair of sandals each.

"Ooh, that's a pretty necklace," Miranda said. "I've never seen anything like it." I touched my neck, I'd completely forgotten I'd left Jennifer's necklace on from the previous night's dinner.

"Oh, this old thing? My mum gave it to me." I said surprising myself, as I never call her mum. Occasionally I sometimes call her 'My mother', but nearly always just 'Jennifer'.

We both made our hair a little more presentable and I followed Miranda out the front door.

She skipped across the lawn and stood out the front of the neighbours' house.

"Mrs Frank, I'm going out with my friend Minky." She called out.

An older lady appeared at the screen door.

"Very well Miranda, you know the rules? Stay away from the Scarba House kids and be home before dark. I'll have some dinner waiting here for you." Miranda nodded.

"Wow, she didn't seem terribly interested in who I was," I said following Miranda as she lead the way down the road.

"She could probably tell you're not from Scarba, so she doesn't care."

"What is Scarba?"

"It's a home for kids, and it's just around the corner. I don't know why my parent's don't like me playing with them," she said with a twinkle in her eye, which made me think she knew *exactly* why they didn't like her playing with them.

SIXTEEN

We headed straight towards the city, with me marvelling at all the differences to the Sydney of today.

Aside from the fact the skyline was considerably shorter than the one I was used to. The thing that stood out to me the most were the cars, it was like we were in one gigantic hot rod show, the only difference was these cars were just old school and didn't have the modifications and flashy lightning bolts and designs on them they had nowadays. Being such a car lover, I couldn't help but think how much Pop would love to see them all driving around Sydney in their original glory.

There wasn't too much traffic on the roads, but Miranda explained there was a lot happening in Sydney that weekend. Aside from the Empire Games, which I had never even heard of, it was a

Sunday so there were the usual sports games and people attending church.

Our first stop was the Botanic Gardens, which was a little different but in a lot of ways felt more like I was back in 2014 than most anything I had seen. The only thing reminding me I wasn't in my time were the people dressed in different clothes.

"Tell me more about your time, what's the future like?"

My mind drew a bit of a blank, but then I started thinking about the contrast between my bedroom and Miranda's.

"Well, pretty much everyone, kids and all have phones they carry around with them everywhere." Miranda looked intrigued which encouraged me to continue. "Most of them are not just phones though, they are smartphones so I guess you could say they are like computers too but they are small enough to fit in your pocket." She looked really confused.

"Computers are machines that allow you to do, well lots of things. My phone, for example, has a calculator, torch, you can play about a million games, listen to music, look at the time or the weather, take photos and check emails, not to mention the internet." Miranda looked really lost now, but at the same time, she looked slightly impressed.

"It's a bit hard to explain the internet, except it pretty much means any information you want is right at your fingertips. The funny thing though is

I'm not sure if having all this information so close at hand is making us smarter or dumber." Miranda seemed to take what I was saying in, but I'm not sure if it made much sense. I guess it's really hard to jump decades into the future.

"What about people in the future? How did you say we are related again? If I'm your great-grandmother, that must mean I end up having children right?" She asked, changing topics to something that was literally a little more relatable.

"Yes, you have one son, who is my pop. I actually live with him now."

"That's incredible. I never even thought I wanted kids, but based on meeting you, I think I now do." I laughed because I also had never thought much about if I wanted kids myself - and if I was honest with myself, I was leaning more towards the side of not going down that path.

"Your son, Robert, my pop, has two daughters Jennifer and Cassandra. *Jennifer* is my mother." Miranda looked at me with a puzzled expression.

"The way you said that makes me think you don't like your mum very much." I screwed up my face.

"I hate her."

"Are you sure Minky? Hate is a very strong word, you shouldn't use it lightly."

"I guess we clash a little, we've never really gotten on," I said feeling sheepish. Hate was a strong word, and as much as we didn't get on, I knew I'd misused the word because I really didn't hate Jennifer. "Do you get on with your mum Miranda?" I asked trying to steer the conversation away from my use of the 'H' word.

"Oh sure. She was a nurse before she got married so she has some very interesting skills and knows so much about ailments, medicine and looking after sick people."

"She sounds wonderful. I'd love to have a mum like that."

"She's a wonderful nurse, but I've heard people say they think she is a bit heartless and cold. I don't think she's ever actually said she loves us, but I just know she does.

"I think she keeps us at arms length a little as it's her way of coping with things she can't control. But she would honestly do anything to help anyone. Even now she has made the long journey by herself to look after my sick aunt. I don't know many people who would drop everything to do that. I think she is quite wonderful actually."

This conversation was making me feel a little awkward. As Miranda described her mother, I started to picture my own. I wondered if our mothers (who did share the same genes after all), were actually more similar than I'd thought. No one could deny Jennifer was a hard worker. Perhaps she had trouble verbalising her love and tried to show it in other ways that didn't translate to me as love.

We'd left the Botanic Gardens and we were getting close to Circular Quay. Every time I noticed something different to 'my day' Sydney, I couldn't help but comment and point it out. Miranda was getting an exceptional insight into what the future would bring.

I wasn't an expert on the buildings in the centre of the city, after all, I had spent most of my life living in Canberra. I knew these days there are a lot of them. The skyline of 1938 was remarkably different to 2014, it wasn't just the height, there was considerably less steel and glass in the 1938 cityscape.

By the time we got to The Rocks, I noticed there were a lot more people out and about on the streets, quite a few were dressed up quite fancy with hats and gloves and I wondered if they'd been to church.

Then there were others who were wearing scrubby looking t-shirts and shorts that looked like they'd never been washed. It felt like Miranda and I were a very happy medium, not underdressed, but not too dressed up either.

When we got closer to the water I could see the iconic Harbour Bridge and it almost gave me a comforting feeling of being home.

"There she is," I said. "It's nice to see that familiar sight."

"It's quite wonderful isn't it?"

"Would you believe they take tour groups up to the top now?"

"To tour the top of a bridge?"

I laughed at her question.

"I guess it's to get the best view of the Harbour. And it is a world-famous icon you know, people would love going back home to say they climbed the Sydney Harbour Bridge."

"Have you ever climbed it Minky?"

"Nah." I shook my head, "we hardly even drive across it nowadays. We normally take the tunnel."

"Tunnel?"

"Yeah, there's way too much traffic for the bridge, so they built a tunnel under the harbour which pretty much goes right under the Opera Hou..." I stopped as I was pointing to the empty space where another iconic building that obviously hadn't been built yet was meant to be.

"What is it?"

"There's another building that usually sits right out there, it's the Opera House. It seems wrong not to see it there though."

"Ooh, an opera house right near the water sounds so lovely. I wonder when it will be built?"

"To be honest, I have no idea. I thought it had been there forever. I really take everything in my time for granted. I really want to tell you though, it is not your classic looking opera house, it's actually shaped like big white sails blowing in the breeze."

I tried looking beyond the bridge, over towards Milson's Point. "Do you know if Luna

Park is around yet?" I asked wondering about the fun park Dad had taken me to a couple of times before Zac was born when we'd been in Sydney visiting Nan and Pop.

"Yes, Luna Park is just over there, but I haven't been to it yet," Miranda said.

"You know where we should go?" Miranda answered her own question before I could ask what she was thinking. "Bondi beach."

"Great idea girl," I said and followed her as she led the way to the train station.

I was surprised to find the trains were not actually trains, but they were trams.

"Wow, this is different, they don't have these trams anymore," I said.

"Why would they get rid of the Bondi trams?" Miranda asked looking like the future made silly decisions.

On the tram ride, Miranda continued asking me questions, many of them prompted me to tell her about the modern conveniences of my day. Some of them made me laugh as I realised as I was talking, in some ways 2014 kind of sounded like we are living in 'The Jetsons' or some other futuristic time even though the future to me is just normal.

I told her about microwaves, digital TV and set-top recorders - which to someone who doesn't even know TV mustn't have made much sense - robotic vacuum cleaners that worked themselves, iPads and Skype, how air travel is so popular, people fly around the world all the time without even giving it a second thought. It made me smile to imagine what Miranda was thinking, but she took a lot of it in her stride.

The conversation seemed to draw a bit of attention from the other passengers on the tram though. Some of the mothers covered their children's ears as if I was polluting their children's minds or saying something blasphemous, but others seemed to enjoy hearing about my crazy and seemingly fictional stories about living in the future.

We arrived at Bondi right on lunchtime and to describe it as hectic was not an understatement. The hot Australian sun was pelting down and prickling our skin. It was the perfect day to be at the beach, and the other beachgoers knew it too.

I was worried about not having a hat or any sun protection to wear, but Miranda laughed at my concerns. It crossed my mind to tell her about the ozone layer or lack of it over our fair land, however, I didn't want to come across as a total doomsday crusader.

I decided to forget the sun smart lecture and convinced her to sit with me in the shade and not out in the pelting hot sun. Miranda bought some fish and chips which we shared while watching the swimmers trying to keep cool in the surf.

"Miranda, there's something I have been wanting to tell you, but I wasn't sure how to mention it." She could no doubt tell what I wanted to tell her was difficult for me to say. "It's about your husband, who I'm guessing you probably haven't even met yet."

"My husband? That's so odd, to think about getting married. I'm only thirteen." Miranda said smiling.

"It's just that, well, he doesn't turn out to be the man you think he is. He… well, he isn't a nice person." Miranda seemed to be seriously contemplating what I was saying.

"But, this man I'm going to marry? I suspect he is the father of your grandfather?" She asked and I nodded to confirm. "Well, I don't think there is much we can do about any of that," she said matter of factly. "If we don't get together, you will never exist."

I hadn't even thought about the consequences of changing events of the past. If I didn't have such a clever great-grandmother I could have wiped myself, my brother, mother, aunty, and pop completely out of existence. Still, if it meant Miranda would have a better life, it might be worth it.

"It's strange to think I'm going to become a wife and a mum. I know it's what all girls are expected to do, but when I thought about what I'd do when I grew up, I always imagined I would do something else. I don't know what exactly, but just be a bit different."

"Oh, don't worry, by everything I've heard about you, you *are* different Miranda. Wonderfully different. I just wish you could have been around when I was born, and watch me grow up," I said glumly. "It was a horrible tragic accident, and I..."

"Shh, Minky, you're doing it again. No talk about my death." She said bravely standing to her feet. "I'm making a pledge right now." She held her right hand over her heart, "I promise to live every day of my life to the fullest. I will take risks, and every opportunity that comes my way." She sat back down next to me, but then thought of something else and stood back up to resume her pledging position. "And I will do my best to love everyone in my life, tell them how much I love them, and never take anyone for granted." I smiled at the gutsy girl, very proud she was my great-grandmother.

"Miranda, I think you're awesome," I said.

"Ha! I don't think 'Miranda' is awesome," she said back. "I wish I had a name as fun and interesting as yours." I nearly snorted my lunch through my nose.

"Minky? You like the name Minky? Minky is a silly name, even for 2014," I said.

"I think it's wonderful. It's different and beautiful."

"I think Miranda is beautiful. It's actually classy and normal."

"Well, it can't be shortened and it's definitely not fun."

"I dunno, I reckon you could shorten it to Manda? Or Randa? Or even something like Miz?"

I said vaguely remembering I'd heard that somewhere before.

"Miz? I love it! I've never heard anything like it."

"You're funny. You have a lovely classic and pretty name like Miranda and you want a zany Minky kinda name like Miz?"

"I still have a bit of money left Minky, wanna go get an ice cream?" Miranda asked.

"You can't go to Bondi without having an ice cream," I replied dreaming about the delectable one I had eaten only earlier that night.

We found somewhere to buy a vanilla cone and even though I was certainly grateful for her generosity, I couldn't help myself and blurted out about the amazing ice cream shop they have in Bondi nowadays, and how creamy and delicious they are.

To anyone else, those comments could have been a slap in the face, but Miranda listened to me describe the interesting flavours with a wistfully dreamy look.

We raced against the sun to eat our ice cream cones before they ended up as big sticky messes all over us.

SEVENTEEN

Our walk took us up to the Bondi Pavilion building, which only hours before I had walked past with Nan and Pop. We stopped right in front of it and I couldn't help but think how little it had changed over all those years, they'd definitely retained the beauty of the proud building.

Looking back towards the water there were red and gold flags flapping around in the breeze right and I had a chuckle that the lifesavers parading around had funny red and gold swimming caps on and their swimmers looked so daggy and old fashioned. They were a far cry from the trendy boardies and blue t-shirts worn by the lifesavers at Bondi these days.

There were quite a lot of lifesavers starting to mill around the bustling beach.

"Why do you think there are so many life-savers at the beach today?" I asked Miranda, "Do you think they are going to do some kind of display or have a race or something?" I was busy watching some of them set up some belt and reels for whatever show they were about to put on. "You really don't see those things anymore."

"Hey, look how far out those swimmers are." Miranda noticed. I hadn't thought anything of it until she pointed it out, but there really were a lot of people who even though they were swimming between the flags, looked like they were a bit too far out. When I say swimming, they were really just bobbing around in the surf to keep cool, but they had definitely been moving further and further away as the tide went out. "They still look like they are only waist deep though." She noted.

"Well, I haven't been able to swim in the ocean without feeling nervous since watching a movie about the Boxing Day tsunami movie in geography class," I said knowing as I said it, it was a stupid thing to say.

To my absolute horror, only seconds after I had said it, Miranda and I both witnessed several huge waves come from seemingly nowhere and crash on top of all the people who were swimming out too far and a large group of them were sucked dangerously out into the ocean.

I screamed and pointed which I'm not sure would have helped or hindered the situation. It was almost like time slowed down and the lifesavers who seconds before had been slowly going about their business were kicked into action and were ready to go.

Both Miranda and I stood there astonished at what was playing out in front of us. There were many people in the water who were obviously shaken up and scared, and they were understandably behaving quite frantically.

I felt a little dazed and helpless, but as I noticed some of the lifesavers returning to the beach with some of the swimmers they had rescued from the sea. It hit me, I could be doing something to help them, rather than stand there gaping at the crazy scene playing out before us.

I ran down to the shore to meet the lifesavers and their exhausted swimmers and started helping them hobble back up to safety so the brave lifesavers could get back out there and bring in more people, Miranda followed my lead. It really felt like aside from the lifesavers, Miranda and I were the only level headed people who were not acting crazy and were keeping calm enough to be of help.

There were people who just needed help getting out of the water, and those who were not in good shape. Some were being resuscitated and I was impressed that for a time without mobile phones, they had sirens blaring on the beach and emergency personnel were already arriving in old-fashioned fire trucks and ambulances remarkably quickly.

Even though things kind of felt like they were happening in slow motion, it didn't seem to take too long for the water to be cleared of swimmers. It looked like the lifesavers had pulled everyone out of the water. The scene on the beach was still pandemonium though. There were a lot of people who were still in shock and some were inconsolable.

The sun was still blazing hot but it had lowered in the sky so I could tell it was now late afternoon.

Miranda and I both decided there was not much more we could do, and the best thing for us would probably be just to go home. It had been such a long day and I certainly didn't want to get Miranda in trouble for staying out after dark.

We wandered back to her house making it there just before 5pm. Mrs Frank noticed us walking past her yard and sung out to us there had been a big drama down at the beach and wondered if we'd heard anything about it.

"Wow, you guys sure do okay in this time without Facebook and Twitter," I said cheekily to Miranda, which would have been another comment lost on her.

We told Mrs Frank we'd been at the beach when it happened, and she looked a little horrified but at the same time, slightly impressed that we knew all about it first hand. She told Miranda to hurry up and get cleaned up so she could tell her all the details over dinner. She also added I should be getting home before my folks got concerned.

"Thank you so much for today," I said changing back into my nightie and out of the borrowed clothes which were now quite sandy and not looking as clean as when I'd put them on. "I remember you saying today was an interesting day for you, now I feel like I know why."

"I will never forget today, as long as I live." She said in a dreamy voice giving me a big hug.

"Boy, I hope they got all the people out safely. Imagine if all those lifeguards hadn't been on the beach, there is no way so many people would have been rescued, especially without jet skis and powerboats."

"Maybe you could stay for a night so you can check the morning newspapers to see if everyone got out ok?" Miranda said hopefully.

"Nah, I'd better get back. I'll just Google it when I get home."

"I have no idea what that means, but I assume it's something you do on your pocket phone," Miranda smiled.

"Miranda, it is so wonderful and weird that my best friend is my great-grandmother, who lives in a different place in time," I said hugging her again.

We returned to the lounge room where I picked up the radio from the future and sat down in the well-worn chair.

"Love you," I said thinking about the shop and everyone back in 2014.

"Love you too." I heard as the light flashed and I felt the dizzying movement again.

EIGHTEEN

I arrived back in the shop as if I had never left. It was still just before dawn with the slightest hint of a glow of light coming in through the window.

I felt a lot more composed than I had the first time I'd travelled and returned. I took a deep breath and stood up carefully, checking the chair to make sure I hadn't left anything behind. I then tiptoed back upstairs, successfully avoiding both of the pesky creaky steps. I gently placed the radio back into its spot on the shelf making sure to tuck the power cord in behind it.

When I was safely back in my bedroom I flicked my computer on. Yes, it was still ridiculously early, but I had to check to see if everyone had survived the beach drama.

I quickly discovered the incident had been called 'Bondi's Black Sunday' and by the accounts

I saw online, it was still to date, the largest surf rescue on record.

I was sad to learn five people had actually died. Four of the people who had been pulled out of the water that day, and then a fifth whose body was recovered later. Thinking about some of the people who were extremely upset on the beach it made sense, I felt bad for the families who had lost loved ones. Still, having been there to witness the events, I had a newfound respect for the Bondi surf lifesavers, their focus and determination to save everyone and not stop until the job was done.

I guess it wasn't surprising there wasn't all that much information about the event on the internet. It happened so long before the internet was even thought of, but I did spend a long time looking for stories and articles about it, and for the most part, I felt they were true accounts to the actual event.

It wasn't long before my bedside alarm went off, scaring me back to the reality that it was a school day and I realised sheepishly I had barely slept a wink. To add to the tiredness and make matters worse, had walked a good lap around Sydney in someone else's sandals and dealt with dramas and excitement of a big beach rescue.

If it wasn't for the adrenaline I'm sure was still pulsing through me, I would have been ready to jump back into bed and sleep all day.

Nan poked her head in my room and laid out my freshly ironed uniform on my bed.

"You better jump in the shower before Pop beats you to it." She said. "I'll make you a takeaway breakfast while you're in there."

I hauled myself into the shower and as I dressed, I could hear Seshna chatting happily to Nan about what she had done on the weekend.

I grabbed the vegemite on toast and the lunch Nan had very kindly packed for me and gave her a peck on the cheek on my way out.

Seshna and I quickened our pace to make sure we wouldn't be late, but we were cutting it fine.

"You look a bit sunburnt Minky. I hope you prepared for the big presentation today and didn't spend the weekend sun baking."

I stopped walking and went cold but at the same time, I could feel my face going a brilliant shade of beetroot over the top of what I realised was sunburn from my time travelling adventure.

"Shoot."

"Minky, no," she said. "Please tell me you have something?"

"Well, big waves are a natural disaster right?" I asked hopefully, "maybe I could talk about Black Sunday since it's all so fresh in my mind." Seshna shook her head and gave me her psycho eyes look.

"You are honestly, the most unprepared, scatter-brained person I know Minky Robinson. And anyway, wasn't Black Sunday a bushfire event? What does that have to do with big waves? Girl, I think you've finally lost the plot!"

I was confusing my friend, but I was also doubting myself. To say I was lethargic and in need of a good sleep was an understatement. Perhaps I could get out of this mess by feigning an illness and going home sick? With my level of tiredness and my sore sunburnt skin, saying I was sick was a half-truth anyway. One thing I knew for certain was I was definitely not in the right state of mind to stand up and do a presentation, but there wasn't time to really get out of it because first class for the day was geography.

"Welcome to class girls," Mr Young said as we found our seats, "I was beginning to think I should have sent you a gold-edged invitation to get you here this morning. Haven't you heard being fashionably late is now passé?"

Cormack was already up the front of the classroom, setting up his laptop and projector for his fancy presentation. He shot me a terrifying glare before he launched into his 'Boxing Day Tsunami' presentation with footage and everything from the event.

As much as I wanted to hate it, he did a really good job and even though a couple of the other guys made fun of parts of his presentation, I could tell it was more out of jealousy rather than because it was bad.

Even though Cormack was a Merrett and more than a little bit annoying, I had to hand it to him, he could give a damn good presentation. Watching him up there, I could actually imagine him as one of those suave politicians who could talk their way out of a scandal.

Instead of daydreaming about Cormack Merrett's future occupation, I should have been thinking about my own presentation and exactly what I was going to say.

I knew compared to my level of preparation, Cormack's talk was going to make mine look like a brown paper bag next to a high tech lunch box. As Cormack received a polite applause from Mr Young and the class and was packing up his props and equipment, I sat silently praying I would not be called next and said a quick prayer to God that if he really loved me, he would give me another day or even two to prepare.

"Thank you Cormack, although you did go over the six-minute limit, you gave a very interesting presentation and showed us you were extremely well prepared." He turned to face the class, "Minky," he said cheerily. "Up you hop." Why God? "Hurry up please Minky, we need to get through ten presentations today."

I nervously took my position at the front of the classroom with no props, not even a piece of paper with notes. I was wishing myself to be anywhere but that place at that point in time. Unfortunately, it didn't work. I knew I needed a token and a travelling chair to do a transporting trick, longing to be somewhere else wasn't going to work.

Most of the class looked uninterested and bored, some looked relieved it was me and not them, but Cormack, was sitting up proudly wearing a smug smile and an eyebrow raised that seemed to say good luck following my awesome show.

"Uh, I'm really sorry I don't have any photos or footage of my disaster to show, but I hope I can tell the story well enough for you can picture what happened," I said hearing the nervous quiver in my voice.

"Yawn." Someone up the back of the room called out and everyone seemed to laugh.

"That's enough." Mr Young said. "Minky, please speak up and tell us what you are going to talk about."

I cleared my throat and with as much confidence as I could muster, I told my class about the Bondi Black Sunday events of 1938 and how, if the lifesavers had not been on the beach that day, there would have been an extreme loss of life. I even told them a bit about how life was back then, how much Bondi had changed and how we are pretty lucky because we still also have a lot of the good stuff including the dedicated and amazing lifesavers.

The more I talked, the more my nerves dissipated and I noticed that even though I didn't even have one prop or display for my presentation, the class actually looked interested and didn't make any more comments or even a peep.

Mr Young looked quite pleased, as I quietly returned to my seat when I'd finished, but he mostly looked surprised. "Who told you about this event Minky?" he asked.

"My great-grandmother was actually at Bondi when it happened, and well, I feel like I experienced it too."

"I think we would all agree you gave an excellently detailed account of an event I hadn't heard about before, I for one felt like you told it as if you had been there." Mr Young said. "A very original event, and good presentation. You've even given me some homework to research tonight."

I couldn't hide the grin from my face. Seshna shook her head with a smile, silently letting me know she didn't know how I'd managed to pull it off so well.

Cormack looked a little bit like someone had laced his water with lemon. He didn't look impressed that someone else received feedback more favourable than his - and I hadn't even had any of his flashy props and visual effects.

It was super hard to concentrate for the rest of the eight presentations which included four about the 2011 Japanese earthquake and subsequent tsunami, another one who dared to take on the same 2004 Indian Ocean tsunami production Cormack had presented (and didn't come close) and three about the 2009 Black Saturday bushfires in Victoria.

My body ached from tiredness, but I managed to easily get through the day because I was floating on cloud nine. I couldn't wait to get home and tell Nan and Pop all about my fluke presentation.

Nineteen

I entered the shop through the front doors ready to burst about my day, but as soon as I did I could hear Pop with a customer so I contained myself and tried to hide my excitement.

"I think we have exactly what you're looking for." Pop was leading a man up to the back corner of the store. "Unfortunately, I don't know the history of the chair, it just sort of came into our possession, but for your purposes, it sounds like it will be perfect."

The word 'chair' was resonating in my head and the hairs on my neck stood on end as I knew straight away they were talking about *my* chair.

I could see Pop removing the white sheet and unveiling my chair to the potential customer.

I couldn't let the chair be sold. This was an emergency.

"Stop! Wait!" I yelled, pushing and weaving myself through the mess towards the men in a fight to keep my chair. "You don't want this old thing, the leather is all worn and even torn in places. It's so ugly it should be on the scrap heap. You don't want to pay good money for this old pile of junk."

The customer eyeballed me with a look of confusion, but mostly like he was thinking I'd just escaped from an asylum. His gaze moved from me to the chair and when it really came into focus, he broke out into a wide grin.

"I have looked in every shop in Sydney and surrounds. This chair is exactly what I'm after."

"No!" I said with more urgency in my voice. I dropped my school bag on the ground, pushed past the men throwing myself onto the chair and trying my best to use my body, arms and legs to cover and protect it from them.

"Minky, what are you doing? You're embarrassing us both." Pop said under his breath giving me the crazy confused look before loudly announcing, "this man is the set decorator for the new Baz Luhrmann movie."

I loved Baz Luhrmann and I loved all his movies and disappointedly I knew the chair was most likely exactly what the set designer needed to decorate a Baz type movie set.

However, there was no way I was going to let this chair go now without a fight. I did what any girl would do if she was a situation like this. I'm not saying I'm proud of myself for it, but remember, I was extremely tired and I'd been on a massive emotional time-travelling, presentation-giving lack of sleep roller coaster. I knew if I couldn't turn him off buying the chair, I was going to have to turn it on.

I clung to the chair as tightly as I could and burst into a deluge of sobbing tears. Both men took a step backwards away from the chair and looked extremely uncomfortable.

Through my award-winning monster tears and while snorting back my running nose in the most unladylike fashion, I came up with a story about how much I had been missing my mum and that I had been coming down here every day to sit in the chair and think about her and how now I felt like it was my last connection to her.

The men stood there gaping in shock for what seemed like ages before Pop said.

"I do have another chair over here, not the same style or character, but it might do the trick."

Pop lead the set decorator to the second chair option through the maze of furniture and goods.

As he was walking away, the man gave one last brave glance back towards me which I am sure was his way of printing my face into his brain so he could ensure to avoid any future exchanges with me. Funnily enough, it's not the first time someone has given me a look like that but I won't go into that here.

I don't think Pop managed to sell him the other chair, as it wasn't long before he was standing back in front of me and this time he was alone.

I was still protectively guarding the chair, but I had started to try and compose myself and wipe away the snot and tears. In an odd way I can't explain, I don't think the sadness and the tears that had come so easily were only for show.

I was feeling sad, and the thing that scared me most was I really did have the weirdest longing to be with my mum. It was a feeling I had never experienced before.

"Minky, your Nan and I are very aware of how hard it is for you to be away from your brother and parents." Pop said, giving me a slightly awkward side hug and rubbing my shoulder. "I'm a little confused with the chair connection, but if you say this chair helps you with your homesickness, how about we move it up to your bedroom? It won't get sold if it's safely upstairs."

A flood of relief came over me. It was so odd that the very chair I had spent months being afraid of and avoiding was now something I couldn't bear to be parted from. I hadn't imagined the chair could be part of my very own furniture, in my very own room, but the thought now made me exceptionally happy.

"Oh Pop." I gave him a big hug, and most likely covered his shirt with my residual tears and mucus. "You're the best."

Pop made a special call to ask Col to come over and help him bring the chair upstairs and to my delight, good ol' Col was there within the hour. Between the three of us, we somehow got the heavy old chair up into my bedroom just in time to wash up and have dinner. Nan had made one of her signature dishes, fried chicken, creamy mashed potatoes, veggies and gravy, so it was easy to convince Col to stay and eat with us to thank him for his furniture moving work.

They talk about comfort food, and this dinner fit the bill. I excused myself after dinner and dishes and retreated to my room with my lovely new furniture addition. Leaving the old friends noisily chatting and laughing in the dining room.

To say I was exhausted was an understatement. It was still playing on my mind that those fake tears had turned into real ones. Was I really missing my mother, or was it more Dad and Zac?

I was enjoying lying on the bed and looking at the chair tucked safely in my room. I really hadn't gone to much effort to give the room my own touch. Maybe subconsciously I didn't feel like I could settle in anywhere without my family?

The bedside clock read 6:43pm but my eyes were so tired they wouldn't stay open a second longer.

TWENTY

I woke up exactly where I'd left, on top of my single bed covers with my school clothes still on. Nan or Pop had obviously been in to check on me, as I had one of the blankets from the lounge room over the top of me. The clock read 2:28am.

The first thing that came to mind was Jennifer. I knew it would be a half decent hour in Dubai and I wondered if she would be up for a chat?

I grabbed my mobile and sent her a quick text: "Hi J, can't sleep. Wonder if ur up 4 a skype?"

Not wanting the rest of the house to be woken up by loud text messages in the middle of the night, I made sure to turn my phone to silent. About two minutes later the room was lit up with the silent incoming message. "It's crazy here. Try to sleep now, I'll call next weekend. M."

Next weekend? So unbelievable, but yet so typical of my mother. I don't know why she'd even bothered to have children in the first place. I knew it would have been my dad's idea to have us and she would have reluctantly gone along with it to make him happy. Sometimes it felt like Dad was a single parent who just happened to be in a relationship.

The only time I could ever remember her even showing anything resembling motherly love to me was when she gave me her necklace right before they left for Dubai. I thought again about that moment and how in my hormonal teenage defiance, I had rolled my eyes and rudely shoved the gift in my pocket.

As a further slap in the face to her, at the airport, I had hugged my dad and brother and told them both I would miss them, and promised to talk soon and regularly. Then I gave my mother a cold salute and said, "All the best to you Jennifer, hope it all works out well."

It seemed like neither of us had ever known how to show love to the other, but I sort of felt bad now because deep down I did think she had been trying.

Sneaking out of bed I found the necklace in the top drawer of my dresser and I noticed the silly thing had already become tarnished again. I was going to have to ask Nan what she did to get the necklace looking so good the other day, although maybe it wouldn't be worth the effort if it was going to keep getting black and tarnished so quickly.

I wasn't sure what was wrong with me, and why I had such an urge to be with my mother, but I knew I wanted to try to use the necklace as a token to see her.

Remembering the embarrassment of turning up in 1938 wearing a nightie, I looked down at my Stone Park school uniform, the shirt now all creased from sleeping in it.

Okay, call me lazy, but I couldn't be bothered changing. It was a lot more presentable than turning up somewhere in night attire I reasoned to myself.

I didn't even know if the necklace would work as a token to visit my mother because I still had doubt about its true history. So I only bothered to shove my feet back into my school shoes, so I wasn't shoeless before sitting down on the chair.

As if it was ready and waiting for me to do exactly that, the chair swept me away quickly with the familiar feeling of travelling and then the heavy clunk of landing.

Twenty One

I blinked opened my eyes and looked up from the necklace in my hand and tried to figure out where exactly I was. The chair had arrived in a lush green park and was sitting under the shade of a large leafy tree. I wasn't sure of the time, but it felt like it was afternoon.

The surroundings seemed familiar to me, but it wasn't until I saw a sign that read 'Haydon Allen building' along with a little ANU symbol in the corner that I figured out I was on the campus of the Australian National University in Canberra. I only knew this because it was the university where my parents had met.

When I was a kid and before my brother was born, my Dad used to take me around Canberra to all the places he enjoyed going when he was younger.

One of the places he liked to take me was his old uni, which was generously spread over a large chunk of the west of the Canberra city centre. I always felt a little daunted and lost when I was there, but he loved to show me the buildings where he studied and all his favourite hang out places. He'd even taken me to a few movie nights and some performances at the Street Theatre, which I had really enjoyed.

Aside from him always gushing about Jennifer when we were on the ANU campus, his other great memory was going to see a band called Nirvana when they played there at the bar. Every time he'd mention it I'd look at him with a "who tha?" kind of look before he'd explain it was the band Dave Grohl was the drummer for before he was in the Foo Fighters. None of that had ever greatly impressed me, but I could always tell it left a big impression on him so I always let him reminisce.

My memories of Dad's stories were interrupted by the sound of a person crying nearby. Interestingly, the students who were walking along the nearby path were showing just as much attention to the girl who was sobbing, as they were to the weird looking private schoolgirl who was sitting in an old decrepit chair under the tree. It was like we were both invisible, almost as if it was an everyday sight and everyone was too cool to do anything but just ignore and walk past.

Approaching the crying girl, I noticed that like me, she was holding something in her hands. As I got closer it became evident it was Jennifer's necklace in the girl's hands.

Funnily enough, it never occurred to me the girl with the necklace was my very own mother who now looked only a few years older than me. My guess would be eighteen or nineteen. To say this was an absolute mind bend for me is no exaggeration.

I racked my brain, but I couldn't for the life of me recall ever seeing any photos or evidence in any form my mother had ever looked like this.

Her hair which I'd only ever known to be styled in a perfect blond bob, was now long and dyed jet black. She was wearing a way too short black dress with purple tights and cherry red Doc Marten boots. To say she had a lot of black eye make up on would be an understatement. Unfortunately, because she was crying most of the eye makeup had run down her face.

The whole scene was quite incredible and on so many levels disturbing. Not only had I never seen Jennifer look like a chick from a dramatic 90s grunge video, but I couldn't recall ever seen her cry before either.

Once I knew for sure it was Jennifer, and maybe because I was so shocked to see her showing a vulnerable side, I had the biggest urge to give her a big bear hug and tell her how much

I loved and missed her. She had no idea who I was, so of course I couldn't.

"Um, excuse me, are you ok?" I asked, touching her gently on the shoulder. It wasn't until I touched her that she looked up at me. "Is there anything I can do to help you?" I asked.

Jennifer was looking really confused and for a moment I thought she had actually somehow recognised me.

"You're a kid," she said, "from Stone Park?"

Damn. I thought, why didn't I change out of my uniform?

"I went to that school, it's in Sydney. What are you doing here in Canberra?" she said sniffing back her tears in a very unladylike fashion and eerily similar to how I had earlier that day when I'd been fighting to keep the chair.

"Oh, um, we're here on an excursion," I said thinking quickly. "We're on a… a bit of a scavenger hunt actually." I noticed Jennifer wipe her runny nose on her sleeve. Wow! What a far cry from her perfect lawyer future self. "So what's wrong? Why are you upset?" I asked.

Jennifer looked back down at the shiny necklace in her hands and the pained look reappeared on her face. Seeing the necklace reminded me that my older version was still in my hand, so I quickly snuck it into my skirt pocket.

"I don't know, I'm just so confused." Jennifer sniffed. "My boyfriend and I broke up. We've been together since I started here and, well, I guess I'd imagined we'd finish uni and get married and that would be that."

My mind was racing. I wondered why she and Dad would have broken up. Neither of them had ever mentioned they'd had a big break up. I guess they'd also never mentioned anything about grunge fashion and dyed hair either so I suppose they had their secrets.

Most of the time if my parents talked about life before me I have to admit I would zone out on them. I'm pretty sure Dad had at least once told me that when he and Jennifer had started going out they knew it would be forever or something soppy like that.

My mother was good at keeping things from me, but I didn't think my dad would lie to me like that.

"I'm sure you guys will patch things up." I awkwardly consoled my young looking mother. I felt pretty confident there was going to be some type of reconciliation here. I couldn't remember my parents ever having a full-blown fight and surely if I existed they must make up and get back together.

Jennifer was shaking her head. "Oh no, that relationship is d-e-a-d. There is no way I will ever get back with that cheating creep. I never want to see him again."

My stomach flipped and I felt a bit sick. Jennifer was a pretty hard woman, but I had never in my life heard her talk like this about my lovely sweet dad. And it was making me nauseous to think Dad could have been unfaithful to anyone. He absolutely doted on Jennifer, even though I didn't think she always deserved it.

"You have to give him another chance," I begged. "I'm sure he is sorry he's upset you this much."

"Upset me? Well, I guess he upset me, but I'm more angry with him than upset."

"You're crying tears of anger?" I asked confused.

"No! These aren't tears for that stupid jerk Jared. They are tears for Matty." It was weird hearing Jennifer call my dad Matty. She never called him anything but Matthew nowadays.

I started to let out a sigh of relief, but then I wondered what might have happened to him and I started to feel worried.

"Um, who's Matty? And is he's ok?"

It took everything in me to hold back from shaking her to find out what was wrong with Dad. She was in such an un-Jennifer like fragile state so I knew if I was going to get anything out of her, I was going to have to be patient and gentle with her.

It hit me that I was going to have to try and help her, and to do this, I needed to know everything about my parents love story, even if it included gory details that I really didn't want to hear.

I was also going to have to stop assuming I knew what was going on and I was going to have to just listen to her talk.

"Matty is, well, he was my best friend here. A few of us at Fenner Hall, we're a close group. Anyway, we met back in the first week of uni and even though we all study different things, we've been there for each other through lots of difficult times." Jennifer sighed, "I considered Matty to be my closest friend here in Canberra and after all the mess with Jared, he was the first person I went to for support."

I was starting to feel relieved. This sounded like the loving and supportive character of the dad I knew. Always a tower of support and a true and loyal friend.

"I was venting to Matty about Jared. Then, with no warning, he pulled out this necklace." She said holding up the delicate chain I was now all too familiar with.

"He gave it to me along with this whole big speech about how much he loved me, and he has always been in love with me, that he watched me fall for Jared and had to patiently sit back, hoping I would figure out what a loser Jared was. He said now Jared and I were over, he wouldn't wait any longer and he couldn't risk me falling for anyone else. Then he professed his undying love for me and said he didn't want to be 'just friends' anymore."

"Then what did you do?" I asked her almost accusingly.

Jennifer looked sheepish and like she might start the waterworks again.

"I laughed." She said.

"Oh." I sighed shaking my head, unable to hide the disappointment in her. I knew how much it would have gutted my dad. He gave her his heart and then she stomped on it so insensitively with her trendy red boots. It took everything in my power not to slap the top of her head to try and knock some sense into her.

"I really don't know why I laughed, it wasn't funny. I think it was like a nervous reaction." The tears and sobbing had started again, so I took a seat on the patch of grass next to her and put an arm over her shoulder.

"I can honestly say, I've never once thought of Matty as more than a friend and I had no idea he had any feelings for me that were deeper than friendship either.

"He looked so wounded when I told him he was more like a brother to me, and that's as far as our relationship could go." She let out a wail. "Oh, the look in his eyes, I've hurt him so much."

I looked at my barely recognisable mother. The woman who was always calm and collected, never rattled or shaken and certainly never ever emotional. I couldn't help but think she actually is human after all.

"Well, I'm not sure if I'm out of line saying this," I spoke up, hoping she would listen. "But do you think one of the reasons you are so upset about hurting him could be because you *are* actually in love with him?"

Weird, young version of Jennifer stopped her sobbing and looked at me with a frown. She seemed to pause for an uncomfortable period of time before she said "You could be right. I think I am in love with Matthew Robinson!"

I let out a long breath of relief. It crossed my mind though, I had to keep some momentum happening and I couldn't risk letting my mother lose the opportunity of being with my lovely dad.

"What are you waiting for then? We have to go after him! Do you know where he went?" I asked jumping back up. If cold-hearted Jennifer was this distraught, I couldn't even begin to imagine how upset my poor sensitive dad would be at this point.

"No idea. I've ruined everything haven't I?"

"Look, I'm going to try and help you find him okay. But you really need to pull yourself together and think about where he could be." I spoke the words to her in a firm voice realising I sounded uncannily like Jennifer's future self.

My firmness seemed to help snap her to attention. She wiped her mascara induced panda eyes with the ends of her poor dirty sleeves, again making me feel like I'd entered another dimension.

"I really don't know. He could be anywhere."

"How about Fenner Hall?" I asked, remembering every time I'd driven past the building with Dad, he would always point it out to me and reminisce about the fact they'd lived 'off-campus' while studying.

Jennifer shook her head. "I doubt it. I reckon he would probably stay clear of anywhere he thinks he might run into me." I nodded thinking it sounded about right.

I racked my brain trying to think of where else he could be when it suddenly hit me and I knew I was on to something. "I know! The merry-go-round. Let's go." I shouted, pulling Jennifer up to a standing position and then dragging her towards the city centre. She looked slightly startled and a little confused but didn't put up a fight. She let me lead her past some of the law firm buildings I knew she would one day work in. We dodged traffic across Northbourne Avenue towards the large merry-go-round.

As we made our way there I couldn't put away the memory of Dad taking me to ride the pretty old carousel in the centre of the city every time we had been in Civic. As I'd gotten older, it had felt like more of an excuse for him to sit and watch, rather than me to have a ride. I could recall him almost looking disappointed when I had said I was too old to ride the horses now.

I'm pretty sure the carousel had been there forever. I know it had been through at least a couple of restorations. It had beautifully decorated wooden horses jaunting gracefully up and down and a couple of stationary elephant shaped seats for kids who were either too young to ride horses or preferred a less adventurous ride. They each had so many layers of thick glossy paint on them, probably a layer to cover each decade of children who had eagerly ridden them.

One of the best parts of the old carousel was the beautiful old organ you could hear around Garema Place playing lovely fairground tunes long before you could see it.

When I was little I loved picking a horse painted in pretty pastel colours, checking out its name printed on the side and pretending I was a princess riding up and down and around and around with the wind blowing in my hair. Even when I had insisted I was too old to ride it, Dad had still dragged me down there to sit and watch the younger kids enjoy the ride. He always seemed to have a funny distant expression as he watched it slowly and smoothly and spinning around. Now I think I knew why. He was remembering something that happened there, and I knew he would be there now, and the following events would be what he would in the future go there to think about.

I couldn't believe how different Canberra looked to the city I had left just over six months ago. I knew there had been a lot of construction work done in the last few years, especially around the university, but I couldn't remember it looking so sleepy, old and tired.

I spotted my poor deflated Dad before Jennifer did, but thankfully I remembered I wasn't meant to know who he was or even what he looked like.

"Well, do you see him anywhere?"

Jennifer looked depressingly through the crowd of nine-to-five workers who had just knocked off and were now making their way to their cars and buses to get home. I was still holding her hand and could tell the moment she spotted him as she tensed up probably from being excited and nervous all at once.

"Yes! You were right. There he is!" She pointed to the extremely young and very cute version of my beloved father who I had never seen looking so miserable. "Oh boy, I don't know what to say to him. I can't do this." She turned to walk away. I knew she would chicken out without encouragement.

"Now you listen to me." I said taking my semi-gothic wimp of a young adult mother by the shoulders and giving her another dose of her future self with my best stern future 'Jennifer' voice. "That guy over there is the best thing to ever happen to you. I guarantee if you give it a go with him, you will be happy for the rest of your life with a man who will bend over backwards to support you and your career, who will do his share and more of the housework and kid raring and he will treat you piles better than you probably deserve."

Jennifer stopped and gave me a kind of hopeful and dreamy look, one I'd never seen on her before.

"Do you really think one day we might have kids?"

Her question absolutely floored me. I couldn't believe my 'career driven' mother, who never seemed very interested in children let alone me, her very own first born child, had the most starry-eyed expression on her face as if being a mother and having children was her lifelong ambition.

If I hadn't seen the dreamy look cross her face and hear her ask the question, I never would have believed it. I was always so sure my dad had convinced a very reluctant Jennifer to have children, I really thought both Zac and I were more of an annoying pothole and speed hump in her smooth sailing high-way of a life.

"Well, I reckon if you want to have kids, there's a good possibility you'll have them." I couldn't help but give her a bit of a goofy smile. "And he looks just like the kind of guy who would make a pretty awesome dad don'tcha think?" She smiled back and nodded.

"Now, he just laid his heart out for you and you broke it. You have to be the one to fix all this." I said giving her a little push in his direction. She replaced her goofy smile with a look of determination and resolve.

"I'm going to go get that man." She said straightening her very short dress and heading through the dark-suited workers towards my dad.

"Go girl," I said.

"Hey, thanks so much kid." She said turning back one last time. "I just realised, I didn't catch your name."

"Minky," I said stupidly without thinking. My mother gave me a look as if she was engraving the name Minky into her brain for future use. My stomach sank as I realised I'd just sealed my own fate with my silly name.

I was the stupid person who gave my mother my ridiculous name when she was at uni. I felt like an utter nitwit. Maybe I could run and correct her and give her a nice different name?

Then I thought about Miranda and how she said she'd love to have my name. I decided to just let it go.

I couldn't help myself but hang around the area for a bit to watch my parents literally kiss and make-up. It was actually sort of sweet and beyond surreal to see them looking so different and young but also very awkward and unfamiliar with each other.

I couldn't hear what they were saying, but Jennifer obviously apologised and Dad being Dad didn't make her suffer for one minute. He very quickly forgave and embraced her straight away. I'm pretty sure I got to witness my parent's first proper kiss as a couple. Just another thing to blow my mind and not really something many kids can (or want to) say.

The thought occurred to me I was still time travelling and I had abandoned my ride home under a random tree at a university. I decided to leave my parents to work out the rest of their lives together and I raced back to where I'd left the chair as fast as I could.

Things were not going in my favour on my return to the chair. It was as if we'd gotten all the green lights on the way to the carousel, but typically I was getting all the red ones back.

Canberra doesn't really have busy peak hour traffic like Sydney does, but there is usually a few moments of craziness as everyone tries to make their way home. I was caught up in the end of day traffic and it felt like I was pushing against an uphill battle.

When I finally made it back to the uni, I wasn't expecting to see what I saw. A huge crowd of students were marching along the generous path leading from the courtyard where all the shops and services are right towards the city. I should have been able to see the chair from where I was now standing, however, there were so many people in the area it was a crazy scene.

I grabbed the arm of someone who didn't look to be all riled up and was minding their business walking past. The guy seemed shocked and slightly annoyed that I was touching him, but turned to face me.

"What's going on?" I asked the stranger.

"Rally against the new mandatory detention laws." He said with a snarl as if I'd been hiding under a rock and should have been aware.

"Oh yeah, right," I said as if I'd understood his explanation although it didn't mean all that much to me. I let go of his arm.

I knew the ANU was a pretty progressive university, and there were a lot of people who were passionate about all sorts of different causes, but I had never seen a protest or rally in the flesh, let alone been right in the middle of one.

The people at the front were holding signs and chanting. I wondered where they were going to end up marching into the city, or if they'd be heading to Parliament House where I assumed these new laws had been made.

Instead of taking the sensible decision to wait for the crowd to pass, I dove straight into the middle of it all, pushing against the angry crowd to try and get to my chair.

Have you ever tried to go against a thick wall of rowdy people who are heading in the opposite direction? It wasn't easy and it wasn't fun.

A large proportion of the crowd had ratty looking dreadlocks and although there was a grungy edge to them, they were a little more hippy than Jennifer's gothic get up. They were also quite on the nose (if you know what I mean?).

If I hadn't received a good workout racing all over Canberra with my mother, I was certainly getting one now pushing against this crowd.

As I approached the spot where the chair had been left, the group of protesters had almost passed and there were a few half-hearted supporters straggling behind the enthusiastic horn blowers at the front.

My gut flip-flopped as the empty spot came into view. I felt physically ill as I looked around desperately for any sign of the chair.

The realisation hit me, I was now stuck in Canberra somewhere in the early 1990s. How was I going to get back home?

TWENTY TWO

I was seriously living my worst nightmare and I was kicking myself for being so blasé about leaving my special chair out in the open for anyone to steal.

How was I going to get back to the right time?

I did like Canberra, and even though some things were the same, it was so different to the Canberra I had been born in.

Even if I was able to get myself back to the familiar surroundings of my old inner north home, my parents didn't own it until a few months before I was born. They were still poor students and were years off purchasing the house.

The thought crossed my mind that I could possibly see if Dad's parents were home. Even though they had moved into a really nice retirement village around the same time Zac was born, I remembered where they'd lived before then and knew they'd lived in the same home since Dad was a kid.

It then occurred to me that the reason Dad lived at Fenner Hall, was because his parents had taken a sabbatical and had spent the year overseas when Dad started uni, so they weren't even living in Canberra.

Anyway, it would have been a pretty awkward situation to try and explain who I was and how I had ended up there.

There was no choice. I was just going to have to find the chair.

I scanned the area and couldn't see any sign of it. I knew it was heavy, particularly since I had only recently helped to lug it up the stairs at Nan and Pop's place. Unless someone had a trailer or some other heavy moving device, it surely couldn't be too far away.

Frantically, I began asking strangers if they had seen a chair. I knew it didn't help that I was getting crazy lady tone in my voice, but I couldn't help it.

Many of them ignored me, but one dude riding past me on a pushbike took his hand off the handlebar long enough to make a gesture with his thumb over his shoulder.

I didn't wait around for further instructions. I took off at speed down the path following his lead towards the shops and then beyond.

Most of the people who had seen it were only willing to provide casual signals like the guy on the bike. It really shocked me it could have gotten so far away in what seemed like not a very long time.

I'd now crossed, over a bridge and a road, but was still on the sprawling uni campus. I was starting to lose light, the temperature had dropped a good few degrees and the Canberra chill I knew all too well was in the air. The campus was feeling a lot less busy and the shadows now more than a little intimidating.

I ended up hearing them before I saw them. It sounded like a handful of guys and they were kind of arguing among themselves.

"This is your worst idea yet JD. Why do we let you talk us into these hair-brained ideas?"

"It's not even that great a chair."

"Yeah, and how come out of the three of us, you've carried it the least?"

The path had lighting, but it wasn't very bright. It made it quite easy for me to stay out of their sight while I assessed who had stolen my chair and what I was up against.

There were only three of them, but in their tight black jeans and flannelette shirts, they looked like clones of each other. I was actually surprised that guys like this even went to uni, they looked less academic and more heavy metal rev heads. Then again, who was I to judge? I'd just had an experience with my rebellious teenage mother who I know turns out to be a very respected and intelligent lawyer.

Two of the guys looked ready to dump the chair and leave it, but the third one was adamant he needed it.

I continued to lay low, hoping the guys who were sick of dragging it around would win the argument and I could reclaim my chair and be on my merry way home.

"Why are we bothering with this ugly old chair anyway?" The tallest of the three said.

"I was thinking we could sell it and get some money for it." The short one who seemed like the ringleader said and the other two laughed.

"Well, if you're not going to help me, then maybe we should have a bit of fun with it." He said taking out a lighter from his pocket and flicking the flame, obviously trying to save face with both of them poking fun at him.

My gut reaction was to run out and stop him as I thought he was about to set it on fire. I was glad I hadn't when he pulled out a packet of cigarettes and lit one of them without harming the chair.

"Now you're talking. Been a while since we had a bonfire on campus," the dopiest of the three said and then I realised my first gut reaction about what his intentions were, were actually founded.

"We should get some tinnies and some other guys to come join the party."

It had me fuming to think these imbeciles were planning on needlessly damaging someone else's property just for fun. Somehow I managed to stay put, but my blood was starting to boil. If they were going to get their nincompoop friends though, then they might abandon the chair for a couple of minutes and it would be plenty of time for me to get myself back to the future and out of the crazy 90s.

"Why don't you guys go get the drinks and some hot chicks and I'll stay here and mind the goods." The annoying short one said falling back into the chair and taking a long drag of his smoke. And then, because the other two weren't moving, he held out his packet of smokes and let the others take one I guess for payment of their inconvenience.

"Hurry up, don't be long. 'Baywatch' is back on tonight." He said making a rude, squeezy gesture with his hands that made me roll my eyes further back than I ever had before. Who the heck was this guy?

Soon the two goons had left and it was just the smoking loser, my chair and me hiding behind a bush. I knew I was going to have to make a move before there was a chance he somehow managed to time travel with the cheap plastic lighter he was throwing up in the air, although I did have strong doubts there was much in the way of intelligent thinking going on upstairs.

I rallied up all my confidence and tried to keep myself as cool as I could when my whole body was shaking.

"Uh, excuse me, that's actually *my* chair," I said leaving the safety of the hiding spot and startling the guy at the same time. I guess he wasn't expecting a kid in a fancy private school uniform to pop up in front of him claiming the chair.

"Get nicked kid. As if it's your chair. Anyway, why would you leave it in the middle of nowhere if you actually wanted it?"

"I had an errand to run, and I knew I wouldn't be long."

"I had an errand to run." He mimicked me cruelly. "How'd you get it there in the first place? And how do you reckon you're gunna move it from here?" He smirked blowing a stream of his cigarette smoke straight into my face.

This jerk was really starting to fire me up. Who did the half-wit think he was? Blowing smoke into a child's face like that?

"If you think you're going to make a bonfire out of my chair, you have another think coming. I'll have campus security here faster than you can blink."

"Oh yeah? How are you going to do that?" He asked getting to his feet and standing over me to no doubt try and intimidate me.

"My phone," I said patting my jacket pocket which aside from a couple of bits of lint and a tissue was actually empty. The guy doubled over with laughter.

I wasn't sure, but I suspected then, that even if mobile phones were invented back then, it was probably not a common thing for young school kids to be carrying them around.

"Look kid. I'm not a total monster." He said letting his laughter dissipate. "I'll tell you what. If you can move this chair to… wherever it is you want to take it, I won't set it on fire when my mates get back." He gave it a fancy game show arm wave as if he was offering me a prize although he did it in complete jest as he knew I would never be able to budge it.

It wouldn't be long before the other drongos were back, and if they were drinking alcohol and playing with fire, I certainly didn't want either myself or the chair to be anywhere near their vicinity.

I had one chance to get us to safety, and there was no chance of him not witnessing it.

"Okay," I said slipping past him quickly and sitting down on the chair that was vaguely warm from his behind. "But before I move the chair, I want to show you a magic trick. You'd better stand back a bit for this."

Ignoring my warning, he defiantly stood his ground. He took one last drag of his smoke before flicking the still lit butt off into the dark night and crossing his arms in front of himself. I could tell he felt like he had the upper hand and it was going to be a win-lose situation in his favour.

I fished around in my shirt pocket and was relieved to find the necklace.

"Um, okay, I'm going to need you to say abracadabra," I said nervously but with as much guts as I could muster.

Unbelievably he played along, but I was already thinking strong thoughts about the safety of my bedroom and being back in 2014. I only heard him say "abra…" before the flash occurred. I did think I saw a quick glimpse of his shocked face complete with eyes bulging out of his head before the light completely swallowed me up and I felt the thud of landing.

I was back.

Twenty Three

It was still the middle of the night, only moments after I had left. My bedroom should have been quite dark, but I noticed it was lit up with a soft glow coming from my bedside table.

The phone I'd put on silent was glowing and vibrating softly. I raced over and picked it up. The screen showed the word 'Jennifer' and displayed the most unflattering picture I had found of her to put against her contact name. I quickly swiped to answer the call.

"Mum?" I asked softly.

"Minky?" she asked with a surprised voice, "I was worried about you, you never try and contact me, especially not in the middle of the night there. Sorry, I couldn't talk before, is everything ok?"

"Yeah, it's all good. I think I was just missing you." There was silence on the other end and I wondered if she was thinking I might have been playing some kind of trick on her. "What are you up to?"

"I'm actually now on my way home from the office, so I have you on the car phone. When your text came through I was wrapping up a meeting so I couldn't talk."

"Mum, you work way too hard. I think you should spend some more time with Dad and Zac. Even though they are over there with you, I'm guessing you see me almost as much as you see them." I heard her sigh heavily in agreement.

"You know, you're right Minky. I do have to cut down on work and reprioritise my life. When did my little girl get so wise?"

"I think I've been growing up a lot in the last few months Mum."

"I'll have to thank your Nan and Pop for doing such a good job looking after you. But you need to know, Minky Robinson, you have always made me very proud."

"Well, at least I haven't dyed my hair black and become a goth or anything crazy like that," I said with a cheeky tone.

"Oh boy, what have they been telling you?"

"Mum? Thanks for calling me."

"We'll have to make it more regular like you do with your dad."

"Yes, that'd be good."

"I should let you get back to sleep now. It is almost 8pm here, so I imagine it would be around

3am there. It is good to hear from you though, so just remember, anytime you need to talk, let me know ok?"

"Will do. Thanks Mum. Oh, and look after our boys okay?"

"Minky?"

"Yeah?"

"I really like it when you call me Mum."

Twenty Four

I'd like to think I had it in me all along. I'm sure I probably did, but I think it was the time travel, and meeting Miranda and I guess also discovering my mother was actually human and standing up for myself against a nasty bully. The strangest thing occurred. I started getting A's in school.

Okay, I had received an 'A' or two before then, but only ever for physical education, never for anything else.

My first 'A' came from my geography presentation which Seshna reckons still gives her the chills when she thinks about how well I managed to do with zero preparation. The teacher had been so impressed he asked if I would repeat my presentation to a whole school assembly.

I felt a little odd about it, but it ended up going really well. The weirdest thing was I think the other teachers and students thought I was someone more confident than I'd ever felt. Most of them hadn't known me, so this was who they thought I'd always been and in a lot of ways it just felt right.

Having done the whole school presentation, I started getting recognised in the halls. People I had never seen in my life would say hi and knew my name. It was sometimes daunting, but also quite nice.

I'd become a little obsessed with researching everything I'd seen and done when I'd been time travelling.

The reason the Opera House wasn't there in 1938 was because the construction didn't even commence until 1958, and it must have been a complicated build because it wasn't completed and opened until 1973.

The Bondi trams, which I had found so much fun and very convenient, were sadly decommissioned in 1960. I was also fascinated to find out, the Empire Games where Miranda's brother and dad had been, were actually what we know today as the Commonwealth Games.

Along with my own research, I often found myself quizzing Pop and sometimes Nan about Miranda. Pop had heard the Bondi story so many times when he was younger, that he was able to tell me the events almost as well as I had told the class, and I'd been there.

I knew I was playing with fire, but I really wanted to know if she'd mentioned me at all. The best I could get out of him was that she was with a 'friend' that day. He didn't remember the friend's name and didn't think she'd ever mentioned it.

Things were still not great with the Merrett twins, it was almost like the more popular I got, the more they despised me. Kayla even found a way to kick me completely off the hockey team, but to be honest, after filling in for Honora as goalie, the game was never going to be the same for me.

My English teacher told me I was good at telling stories so she encouraged me to write. I wrote her some stuff about how people can be complex and we think so much about ourselves, we never really know what other people have been through and how it makes them behave. She went nuts about it and made me join an after-school writing class, which replaced the hole in my schedule due to my dismissal from the girl's hockey team. It shocked me how much I enjoyed putting words down on paper, and it got me thinking I could even write some stories about the chair, pure fiction though of course.

Even my mathematics improved if you can believe it. I'm not up to 'A' grade yet, but I'm doing better than ever before and I secretly wonder if it's due to all the hours I've spent working out times and dates from my travelling adventures.

I finished term three of the school year on the biggest academic high of my life.

Pop was over the moon ecstatic because the Rabbitoh's had made it straight to the preliminary finals.

My mum had even started cutting down on her work hours and was spending more time with Dad and Zac. Even though I only had the chance to talk to her once a week, it was now regular and it often ended up being the same time I Skyped Dad because she'd been working way more sensible hours. It was actually quite nice to see them squeezed onto the screen together. I felt a bit like I knew some of their secrets and their relationship history, and every so often I caught a little glimpse of the teenage version of them even though they were now both aged in their early forties.

Mum showed no signs of recognising me from her uni days and I wouldn't be surprised if it was due to the amount of black mascara she had clogging up her poor salty eyes that day.

Life would have almost been close to perfect if I didn't have the guilt about Miranda hanging over me. I just wished there was a way I could prevent her from all the bad stuff from happening to her. If I could figure out how to go back one last time to warn her about her death.

Even if I could somehow mention the fire so she could avoid being at that hotel, at that time. She would be old, but she might still be here living with us all today. No amount of mathematics could solve this problem for me.

I searched the house looking for anything that could have been Miranda's so I could try and travel back to warn her. I racked my brain thinking about things she had said or done to give me a hint about what I should look for, but I came up with nothing.

So although all these great things were happening in my life, I still couldn't help but feel a loss, and like I had really failed my best friend Miranda.

TWENTY FIVE

On Sunday, 5 October 2014 the South Sydney Rabbitohs won the NRL grand final with an impressive score of 30-6 against the Canterbury-Bankstown Bulldogs. After 43 years of drought, it was a real celebration and everyone in my family were beyond stoked, including me. I hadn't seen the years of passion Miranda had shown for her dependably unlucky team, but now I had a connection with her, and knowing she was the root of my family's love for the team, it was very satisfying to see them win. I'd never in my life heard the 'Glory, Glory to South Sydney' song sung so incessantly, but I admit, I joined in a few times.

Because we all had a day off for Labour Day, I had one last day of school holidays before I started the final term of my first year at Stone Park. It was hard to believe how far I'd come in such a short time and how fast the year was flying past.

I was in no hurry to get myself out of bed, and Nan and Pop had already mentioned the night before that they would be taking advantage of the public holiday and would head down to Redfern Oval to celebrate with some of their friends and the team, rather than travel up to the central coast to the Hot Rod Sunday breakfast Pop usually never missed on the first Sunday of every month in his Chevy.

By the time I had pulled myself out of bed to eat some breakfast, it was a lot closer to lunchtime than breakfast.

Pop had left the newspaper on the table and it had obviously already been poured over by both of them as it was covered in toast crumbs and coffee stains. Most of the newspaper was filled with stories about the game and how well the boys in red and green had played the day before. It was almost as if there were no other news stories that day. I enjoyed reading about all the people who had followed the team all their lives even though, like my mum, they had never seen them win a premiership in their lifetime.

Page eight contained a stack of small articles and photos of fans who had been to the game or were caught up in the excitement of the win.

One stood out to me because it mentioned one of my favourite things... ice cream. An avid fan who owned a small ice cream shop had created a special strawberry and pistachio flavoured swirl ice cream she called 'Rabbitoh Ripple' in honour of the team.

I recognised the shop in the photo as the little one we'd been to in Bondi, however, in the photo the shop had been completely decked out with decorations and signs to support the South Sydney team. It wasn't easy to make out the lady's face in the halftone newsprint, but the description under the photo made my stomach flip. 'Local lady Miz with her 'Rabbitoh Ripple' ice cream'.

"What?" I said out loud even though there was no one around to actually hear me. It was definitely the lady that had handed me the free ice creams for Nan and Pop at Bondi. I hadn't realised it at the time, but now I knew Miranda better I was adamant it was her. The lady in the photo was Miranda… my Miranda!

I tore the page out of the paper and raced to my room to get dressed. Then I raced downstairs, locked the back door and sped out to the back shed to grab my bike.

A million thoughts went through my mind as I rode as quickly as I could to the beach. Could it really be my great-grandmother? How did she survive the fire? Where has she been hiding for the last twenty-eight years? How did she still look so young?

Bondi Beach was absolutely packed. Not only was it a public holiday but also the last day of school holidays so it felt like all the kids were there to enjoy their last day of freedom for another term.

I felt like I couldn't breathe. Whether it was from the fact I'd ridden down there at crack neck speed or whether it was because I was desperate to believe Miranda could somehow be alive.

There was an impressively long line at the busy ice cream store, and unsurprisingly it was still decorated lavishly in red and green as it had been in the paper. I tried to look past the crowd into the shop to see whether the lady was there working. There were several people working behind the counter, but none of them looked like Miranda.

That's when I heard the voice.

"Are you looking for me Minky?"

Twenty Six

I spun around after hearing my name and to my utter relief there in front of me was my great-grandmother and best friend in the flesh. It was the oldest version of Miranda I had met yet, but surprisingly she still looked pretty spritely (I'd say closer to sixty than ninety years old).

"Is it really you?" I asked in disbelief, tears coming to my eyes. She had a sparkle in her eyes and was grinning widely as I dropped my bike and ran into her arms. We hugged and laughed and jumped and cried until we were starting to get a bit of an audience.

"Oh, we're just so happy about the Rabbitohs win," I said to a couple of people who nodded and smiled awkwardly before moving on.

"How about we go find 'our spot' and we can catch up?" she said motioning over to the area where we had been sitting just before we witnessed the beginnings of the Black Sunday events. For me, it had only been a couple of months, for her it had been decades. "Looks a bit different now days doesn't it?"

"I can't believe this. I mean, I'm so happy to see you, but I don't understand." Miranda gave a chuckle.

"Even though you were the one who introduced the chair to me Minky, it seems I was the first one of us to actually find it."

"The time-travelling chair? You found it? What? Where?"

"Let's see, you possibly know all this but, back in 1980 I decided to retire, so I sold the shop to Robert to get a bit of money and go travelling around the world. I went to some amazing places and saw some really brilliant things.

"I walked the Great Wall of China, went on safari in Africa, rode camels in Morocco, saw the Northern Lights in Norway, I learnt to make cheese in France, and gelato in Italy, I even drove across America in a beautiful old corvette." I shook my head in awe of my amazing great-grandmother and all the incredible things she'd seen, done and achieved.

"I was working my way through the Caribbean with my sights set on exploring Machu Picchu when it happened. I'd arrived in San Juan, Puerto Rico the day before New Year's Eve in 1986. I'd met some people who convinced me to stay and spend New Years with them at a beach party. I had checked myself into one of the more reputable hotels there as a bit of a treat because I'd been staying in some pretty low budget places.

"I was leaving my room on my way out of the hotel to head to the party when the building fire alarm sounded. Even though I was pretty sure it wasn't a real fire, I still did the right thing and calmly walked down the fire stairs rather than taking the lift. When I got down to ground level I tried to evacuate the hotel but the fire exits were locked and I couldn't get out. This was when I started to panic as there didn't seem to be a way out and things were not looking good for me."

I couldn't help but think about how terrifying it would have been for her. I was hooked on every word Miranda spoke. I had of course, already scoured through newspaper articles and the handful of internet stories about the fire, so I knew the hotel management had purposely locked the fire exits because they were trying to prevent the thefts which had been a growing problem in the hotel. I was tempted to tell her some of these details, but I didn't want to interrupt her story.

"There was so much smoke, heat and flames all around, my only option was to head back up the stairs one level. On the second level, there was still smoke, but it was less chaotic than the ground floor. All the calmness I'd initially felt had was gone, I knew I was in dire trouble, I could hear people screaming, crying and it was all complete havoc.

"That's when I saw it through the smoke and the drama… The chair. It had been a while since I had seen it, but I recognised it straight away. There was no doubt it was 'our' chair too because it hadn't changed a bit. I had no idea how it had appeared there, perhaps someone else had travelled on it to that point. I looked around to see if anyone was going to claim it. Even though there was pandemonium in the air, there was not another soul around me. I knew the chair was my ticket out of danger. With everything going on, the only thing I could think to use for a 'token' was the necklace you'd left behind back in 1938." I touched my neck and rubbed the tarnished necklace I'd been wearing every day since my travelling experience with my mum. I felt very confused as to how Miranda came to have it in 1986.

She seemed to notice my confusion so she explained. "It must have come off when you changed back into your nightie because I found it on my bedroom floor the day after you visited me in 1938 and I think I wore it every day thereafter."

"No way!" I said, still a little confused, but with it all starting to make a bit of sense. "That's why it suddenly looked so old and tarnished." I smiled. "I found it down the side of the chair in the crack between the seat cushion."

"Oh, I'm so glad you found it." She said looking relieved. "I'm quite attached to your beautiful necklace you know? I'd worn it every day from the age of thirteen until, well just months ago when it brought me to the future.

"When I was trying to get out of the burning hotel, I grabbed it off my neck and held it in my hands and focused hard on you Minky. I wasn't sure if I was doing it right and I hoped it would deliver me to you. When I arrived in 2014, I figured out pretty quickly the chair had taken me back to my old shop in Newtown. It hadn't changed a bit."

"Hey, when I asked Pop where the chair came from, he said it arrived around the same time I did. Maybe you travelled to the shop on the same day Mum said goodbye and gave me her necklace before she moved to Dubai?"

"Even though I can't explain it, it would make perfect sense."

"I can't believe this. Everyone will be so happy to see you and know you are alive and survived the fire."

"Hang on Minky," Miranda said holding up her hands, "as much as I'd love to see everyone again, I don't think we should tell them about this," Miranda said kindly but sternly. I wanted to argue the case, but I decided she was probably right. It would be too much to explain and way too far-fetched.

"Well, why did you wait so long to let me know?"

"I'm not sure Minky. My first instinct when I arrived in 2014 was to find you, but when I heard other voices, I knew I had to get out of there. As time went on I worked out you hadn't started travelling yet and knew I was going to have to wait for things to play out and for you to find me." She winked at me. "I thought you might figure out it was me the night you bought the ice cream, but you didn't seem to recognise me at all." She said laughing.

"Maybe it didn't occur to me to be on the look out for you because I thought you had died!" I said giving her a playful punch on the arm. "It's funny though, maybe there was some kind of subliminal message in that because it was actually the same night I ended up figuring out how to travel back to 1938."

"We've both come a long way since then girl," Miranda said sounding eerily similar to me. She then pulled a smartphone out of her pocket and waved it at me cheekily. If I hadn't been sitting down, I think I would have collapsed.

"Well, you've certainly embraced the twenty-first century Miz."

"It wasn't hard, I knew what was coming."

We both giggled and hugged again. I couldn't believe I had my best friend back. She might have aged a bit, but we still really got each other.

I sat there taking in the moment. It didn't seem like it could be possible for things to have worked out any better.

Life might be strange sometimes, yes, but why does that have to be bad? I actually think strange can be pretty darn good.

Acknowledgments

Huge thanks and much love to...

My mum who was the first person to hear my 'Minky' ideas and encouraged me to write the story... Then patiently listened and/or read every single draft, version and story idea. You are a saint!

Kat my sister and best friend. Thank you for always being there, leading the way, 'getting me' and sharing your beautiful family with me. You constantly inspire me with how amazing and talented you are. I have always and will always love just hanging out with you - it fills my tank!

Nan and Suzanne. For telling me lots of family stories from the old days... some of which have made their way into this book (even if I have scrambled them up a bit)! And for lots of fun Skyping sessions - not quite as good as being in the same room though.

Elizabeth, Lee and all other members of my book clubs past and present, for encouraging me in my writing and more importantly diversifying and helping me branch out in my *reading*.

Andrew and Bernie for their encouragement, valuable feedback and incredible eye for detail!

Sherri and Pam, lovely ladies who like to lunch with me. Not only do you listen to my stories and ramblings, you seem to enjoy hearing them.

Nike, Jacqui, Nicholetta, Michelle, Mandy G, Mandy S, Sam, Lara and Kate. Just some of my incredible friends who have blessed me for many years with their friendships. We've shared school times, work times, good times and bad, plus some pretty awesome travel adventures! I am definitely blessed with some wonderful close friends.

My precious little Zara. Your arrival may have delayed my writing dreams for a few years, but you'll always be the best and most perfect thing I have ever played a part in creating.

Don't miss Minky's next instalment!!

About the author

Angela Moyle has become slightly obsessed with researching her family history in recent times and since she was young she's had a fascination with books, movies or shows about 'time travel'. She has built houses for *Habitat for Humanity*, assisted in the unexpectedly fast delivery of her sister's baby (on her kitchen floor!), renovated several houses for fun and is still working on completing a full cryptic crossword without assistance... something that has eluded her to date.

Although not fluent in social media she does try to make an effort every now and then.

She lives in a small but extremely comfortable cottage in Canberra, Australia.

www.angelamoyle.com